"Max Van Larsen," Sylvia said, "you're a brute. Now *go!*" He dragged on his cigarette.
"I said *go!*"
"Sylvia," said Max gently.
"*What!*"
"This is my apartment."

By George Baxt:

<u>The Pharoah Love Trilogy</u>
A QUEER KIND OF DEATH*
SWING LOW, SWEET HARRIET*
TOPSY AND EVIL**

<u>The Van Larsen/Plotkin Series</u>
A PARADE OF COCKEYED CREATURES*
"I!" SAID THE DEMON*
SATAN IS A WOMAN**

<u>The Celebrity Series</u>
THE DOROTHY PARKER MURDER CASE*
THE ALFRED HITCHCOCK MURDER CASE*

<u>Non-Series Novels</u>
THE AFFAIR AT ROYALTIES
BURNING SAPHO
THE NEON GRAVEYARD
PROCESS OF ELIMINATION

*now available in a Crime Classic® edition.
**forthcoming from the IPL Library of Crime Classics®

GEORGE BAXT

"I!" SAID THE DEMON

INTERNATIONAL POLYGONICS, LTD.
NEW YORK CITY

"I!" SAID THE DEMON

Library of Congress Card Catalog No. 87-80309
ISBN 0-930330-57-9

Printed and manufactured in the United States of America
by Guinn Printing.
First IPL printing June 1987.
10 9 8 7 6 5 4 3 2 1

For Gawn Grainger

"Up Up and Awayyyyy!"

"I!" SAID THE DEMON

"*My* name is Sylvia Plotkin."

"My *name* is Sylvia Plotkin."

"My name is Sylvia *Plotkin*."

The three nervous women stood in a row on the elevated platform facing the audience, the technicians, three television cameras, four celebrity panelists and the program's host, who, Sylvia thought, resembled her detective (Mine! *Ha!*) Max Van Larsen but couldn't possibly be as stubborn, unreasonable and pigheaded.

(Wherever you are, Max Van Larsen, Sylvia thought to herself, *suffer!*)

"I, Sylvia Plotkin," read the Host in a voice Sylvia associated with her dentist complacently telling her she had two cavities and a loose cap, "am a teacher at Robert Wagner High School in New York City's Greenwich Village. My experiences as a teacher are vividly, humorously and warmly detailed in my first book, *May I Leave The Room?*—which this week reaches the number-one position on the *New York Times* best seller list."

4

(And what is my position on Max Van Larsen's list? Number *nothing!*)

"I am a native New Yorker," continued the Host as Sylvia silently cursed the bead of perspiration tortuously trickling its way down her spine, "and have served with the Board of Education for over a decade."

(*Decade!* Couldn't he say *ten years?* Decade sounds so old, so ancient, so outworn, so historical. And that's what *you* are as far as *I'm* concerned, *my* detective Max Van Larsen. *Ancient history.* Which reminds me, it's time I gave those gangsters in History Three an oral exam.)

The Host hunched forward for a better view of the teleprompter. "Although I have authored a best seller, I have no intention of resigning my position as teacher. To abandon my first profession would be an odious self-betrayal."

(*Odious* and *betrayal,* which only *partially* describes *you* at this very moment, my detective Max Van Larsen. How *dare* you . . . how . . . how . . . Max . . . Max . . . where are you, Max? Is this how it ends? In some future decade will we see each other again across a crowded room? Maybe Bloomingdale's, where I'll be signing autographs, as usual . . . and there'll be a surge of music . . . Tchaikovsky's Fifth Piano Concerto . . . tears will spring to our eyes . . . arms outstretched we'll run to each other. *Max!* We'll be ten years *older!* How much longer, oh Host, how much longer? That trickle of perspiration is turning into a raging torrent and I'm wearing a Balenciaga original.)

Oh Host was not quite finished. "I have completed my second book, a detective novel entitled *The Murder of a Teen-Age Boy* . . ."

(All right, my Max, I'll grant you that. You have a point there. *You* were assigned to find Tippy Blaney. And you found him and his rotten slimy murderer. But why didn't you tell *me* you were writing your *own* book about it? Why must you always be so *secretive?* If I didn't know you were writing a book of your own, what's to get angry? Why, we might even have collaborated. Like Kaufman and Hart. Isherwood and Auden. Loeb and Leopold . . . Why are they applauding?)

The Host's summation completed, the three Sylvia Plotkins descended, as rehearsed, and took their positions at a large desk facing the celebrity panelists.

(I'll never get through the next seven minutes. Never! They must have guessed by now I'm the real Sylvia Plotkin. Max, you miserable Dutchman, I'll never forgive you for last night! *Never!*)

They had lingered over coffee the previous evening after a delicious dinner of steak, salad and low-calorie dressing. There was a small blaze in the fireplace and the charmingly furnished living room had never seemed more cozy. During the brief silence in which both squeezed a drop of Sweeta into their cups, Sylvia again drank her fill of Max. Such a handsome, distinguished-looking man, with his dark blond hair, well-chiseled features Rodin might have admired, trimly muscular body especially for a man in his early forties—and what a catch. Who will weave me the magic net with which to fulfill the deed? thought Sylvia as she cleared her throat.

"Max." He looked up with a quizzical expression. "I have a surprise for you."

Max steeled himself. He was well versed in Sylvia's surprises.

"I've completed another book."

"You haven't!"

"I have." She hoped she sounded properly shy, demure and modest in no particular order. "I'm dedicating it to Tippy's memory."

Max went pale.

"What's wrong? Is it your stomach again? Did you forget your pills?" Sylvia had never seen Max turn albino before.

"Is the book about Tippy?" The words sounded as though they'd been strained through a rusty sieve.

Sylvia tried to control her shaking hand as she placed the cup and saucer on an end table. "Yes," and then as an afterthought, "dear."

Max carried his coffee to the fireplace and stared into the flames. The muscles in his jaw were working, and Sylvia's stomach felt the way it always felt when she was descending in a fast elevator.

"My editor loves it," said Sylvia bravely, her voice a poor imitation of itself. "She wept through the last chapter." Sylvia folded her hands in her lap as she added gently, "The pages are still damp."

Max placed the cup and saucer on the mantel and faced Sylvia. "Why didn't you tell me you were writing this book?"

"There would have been no surprise. You know how I like to surprise you."

"I'm surprised," he stated flatly.

"You're upset." She unfolded her hands and dried the wet palms with her napkin.

"You should have told me."

"Why?"

"Because I've been writing one myself."

For some unfathomable reason Sylvia was instantly reminded of the old magazine advertisement that began *They laughed when I sat down to play at the piano,* and suppressed a giggle which she knew at this moment would have spelled curtains. For want of anything better to say, Sylvia inquired gravely, "Is yours fiction or nonfiction?"

"What difference does it make now?" said Max, groping in a pocket for his pills. "It's all been a waste of time."

"Nonsense!" cried Sylvia, leaping to her feet and crossing to Max. His hand missed her chin by a hair as he popped two pills into his mouth. "I'll withdraw my book," said Sylvia with Nathan Hale bravery.

Max exploded, "For crying out loud! Stop acting the martyr!"

Sylvia's eyes blazed as her face reddened. "Plotkins," she said firmly, "are never martyrs." Max chewed furiously as Sylvia crossed back to the end table and took a grip on the coffee cup. "After all," she continued, "it was your case." She sipped the coffee and strained to keep from choking on it.

In the thirty seconds in which Sylvia gasped for air, Max lit a cigarette and regarded her heaving body contemplatively. "Forget it, Sylvia. If we hurry, we can make the Truffaut at the Bleecker."

"The situation hardly calls for Truffaut," said Sylvia grandly, wondering if Katherine Anne Porter had ever been in this kind of mess.

"There is *no* situation," said Max through clenched teeth. "When two writers tackle the same material, it is obvious the *established* one will receive preferential consideration."

"*Aha!*"

"What's the 'Aha'?"

"I repeat, '*Aha!*' " She faced him with her arms folded. "Established and preferential! The irony in your voice has not escaped me!"

"I simply made an inescapable observation." His voice rose two octaves, traveled eight feet and settled around Sylvia's head like an invisible crown of thorns. "You have written a best seller. You are a money writer. You have written a second book. Your editor likes it. She slobbered . . ."

"*Slobbered . . . !*"

". . . all over the last chapter, which is probably now baking under your hair drier . . ."

"I will not listen to this . . . this infamy!" She crossed to the door and pulled it open.

"You damn well will listen!" shouted Max. "I apologize for my initial reaction. It was unsporting."

" 'Unsporting' he shouts like one of those butchers riding to the hounds!" She was addressing the hallway. "He knows damn well he'd like to wring my neck. He knows damn well that at this very moment he's thinking of me as treacherous and deceitful. He knows . . ."

"Sylvia!" shouted Max, "I'm over here!"

She slammed the door shut and leaned against it, fighting back tears. She spoke slowly and damply. "I'm withdrawing the book."

"I'll never speak to you again if you do."

Oy, thought Sylvia.

"I mean that, Sylvia."

"Max Van Larsen," blurted Sylvia, "you're a brute. Now *go!*"

He dragged on his cigarette.

"I said *go!*"

"Sylvia," said Max gently.

"What!"

"This is *my* apartment."

"All right! All right!" cried the Host, his voice cutting through the audience's laughter. (I made them laugh, Sylvia thought to herself complacently, so maybe my heart isn't all that broken after all!) "That's all the time we have! Now, Panel, you have thirty seconds in which to decide which of these three charming and delightful ladies is the *real* Sylvia Plotkin!"

And the three had truly been charming and delightful. The two ladies surrounding Sylvia were her friends, and they had rehearsed Sylvia's background for three hours prior to the show's taping. On Sylvia's left sat her editor, Edna St. Thomas Shelley, an attractive spinster in her mid-forties. On Sylvia's right sat Chloe Grace, a Greenwich Village landmark who was probably in her early sixties, though her richly hennaed hair and carefully made-up face belied the truth. The three exchanged beaming looks as the panelists carefully marked their cards.

Like the expert bridge player she was, Edna St. Thomas Shelley was false-carding. Her winning smile camouflaged a seething anger. Withdraw her book indeed! Sylvia's got to be kidding. She alone's responsible for next month's fat dividend to our stockholders. And who the hell's this Max Van Whatever? A detective with the Missing Persons Bureau! Lotsa luck! The only detective I ever met could barely thread three words together, and they were "You're under arrest." Of all my authors to act up this week, E.S.T. thought grimly, it would have to be Plotkin. I'll straighten her out. I'll get her a bigger cut on the paperbacks.

Chloe Grace was thinking of her older sister, Ramona. I suppose I should have told her I was going to do this show as a favor to Sylvia. When she sees it, and she never misses it, she'll probably blow her stack and then detonate mine. Oh, what the h. I couldn't resist the idea of being hit by a spotlight again. I wonder if they noticed the way I came down those steps. I haven't forgotten a thing Ziggy taught me. Head up! Shoulders back! Knees stiff and walk from the thighs! When Ramona and I came on together, it always tore the house down. She bit her lip. Tear the house down. That's why Ramona's behaving so strange lately. They're trying to tear our house down. Not our house. *His* house. We can't let them tear *his* house down. It would kill Ramona. It would kill everything.

Max, thought Sylvia, Max.

"All right, Panel!" cried the Host. "Your thirty seconds are up! Now"—his voice taking on the ho-ho quality of a department-store Santa—"who do you each think is the *real* Sylvia Plotkin?"

Panelist number one, who was also an established author, removed her pince-nez and held up her card, on which was printed the number 3.

"I choose number three," she said in a buzz-saw voice as E.S.T. Shelley's eyes widened in surprise, "because she answered all her questions like a pedant." E.S.T. made a mental note to reject her next novel.

Panelist number two, a reformed safe-cracker attempting a new career as a humorist of the Will Rogers school but without a hope of matriculating, held up his card, on which was also printed the number 3.

"I choose number three," he said in a voice that was one part South Carolina and two parts San Quentin, "because she reminds me of my old schoolmarm back in Yokapitee County who used to say, 'There ain't no such critter as a poor chile cuz edjeecashun in this wunnerful country of our'n's is for free and so every chile is therefore rich.' "

The audience chuckled politely, and E.S.T. made a mental note to check his parole board.

Panelist number three, a lady society columnist who was antisocial and alcoholic, held up her card, on which was printed the number 1.

"I choose number one," she said, too slowly and too precisely, "because I think she's in disguise."

Chloe gripped the edge of the desk tightly as she felt Sylvia's hand gently patting her knee.

The fourth panelist, a handsome middle-aged movie star who was facing exile to Europe as a star of Italian cowboy movies, held up his card, on which was neatly printed the number 2.

"I choose number two," he said with a slight British accent, which he had practiced as a teen-aged boy in Flatbush, "because of her sincere and impassioned plea for more schoolteachers" (a smattering of applause) "and her adorable dimples."

The audience roared with laughter, and Sylvia's face lit up like a beacon off Ambrose Channel.

(And *you,* Max Van Larsen, have you ever *once* had a kind word for my dimples?)

"All right! All right!" shouted the Host through the laughter. "Now! Will the *real* Sylvia Plotkin *please* stand up?"

The real Sylvia Plotkin stood up amidst a new burst of applause and then, unexpectedly and for a reason known only to herself, burst into tears.

C H A P T E R **II**

Unaware that some sixty blocks to the north of his precinct Sylvia Plotkin's emotional display was being immortalized on tape, Detective Max Van Larsen of the Missing Persons Bureau sat behind his desk in his office staring at a blank sheet of paper in his typewriter. A name was skipping rope in his head.

Judge Kramer.

Max's eyes traveled to the legal pad on which he had jotted numerous notes.

Name: Armand Mathew Kramer.

Born: New York City, September eleventh, eighteen hundred and eighty-seven.

Disappeared: July twenty-eighth, nineteen hundred and thirty-two.

Disappeared with him: approximately two hundred and forty thousand dollars in either cash or negotiable bonds.

Left behind: one wife, Lita Swenson Kramer, self-styled prima donna (mezzo-soprano, and according to at least three accredited critics, bordering on the baritone) with the Puccini Opera Company.

Puccini Opera Company: Impresario, Signor Ezio Puccini. Company officially disbanded three weeks after Kramer's disappearance. Chief source of funds for the Puccini Opera Company, reputed but never proven, Judge Kramer.

Kramer's associates: all rumored but never proven, three notorious gang lords ("Eyes" Ruby, "Six-Finger" Finestine, "Rightie" McGurk); one crooked attorney, Morgan Montescue; one mistress, Nola Kemp of the Ziegfeld Follies.

Gone But Not Forgotten: "Eyes," "Six-Finger" and "Rightie."

Untraceable: Morgan Montescue, Nola Kemp.

Traceable: Lita Swenson Kramer, Signor Ezio Puccini.

True Mystery Magazine: offering Max Van Larsen fifteen hundred dollars for an interesting, in-depth, fast-paced and witty article on the disappearance of Judge Kramer.

Max Van Larsen: damn you, Sylvia Plotkin.

With a sigh of disgust Max pushed the legal pad aside, swung the swivel chair around and stared out the window into the playground across the street.

The cold October sun haloed around the Pied Piper on a campstool entrancing an audience of about a dozen youngsters, ranging in age from six to fourteen, sitting on wooden boxes in a semicircle. How easily he drew the children to him. How deftly he enchanted them with fairy tales, legends and simple ghost stories. How simply and eloquently he differentiated the characters for the youngsters, eliciting laughter, squeals of fear and cries of "Another one! Tell us another one!" If Max were an artist (and the future purchase of oils and canvas was in the back of his mind), what a stunning subject the Pied Piper would make.

The Pied Piper was a hulking six-footer, but he moved with an amazing grace and nimbleness. His head bore the weight of a massive bush of red Harpo Marx curls. His face was covered with an immense red beard that was always immaculately trimmed and combed. All that was visible was a bulbous nose and two kindly, twinkly agate-blue eyes.

He had materialized in the neighborhood some eight or nine months ago, promenading through Washington Square Park, tootling on a pennywhistle, and in no time at all, like the legendary Pied Piper, he was followed by a line of children. His storytelling followed, and very soon news of his delightful presence reached the ears of the one and only Sylvia Plotkin.

It was Sylvia who arranged for his position as custodian at Robert Wagner High School. It was Sylvia who arranged for a basement storeroom converted into living quarters for the gentle old man. Max was convinced he was either in his sixties or seventies, but he had the vigor and strength of someone twenty years younger. It was Sylvia who saw to it that he had a new warm coat for the winter and at least one hot meal a day. He was Sylvia's special property, and very early she made it clear that anyone who treated him with disrespect would answer to Sylvia. And everyone knew better than to have to answer to Sylvia.

On occasion Max had stolen a few minutes and joined the children and was briefly transported back to childhood again, and his grandmother's tales of the old country. He, too, had his favorites of the Pied Piper's repertoire. He liked especially the one about the fairy princess abducted by a demon in disguise. And when the fairy prince cornered the villain in an enchanted cave and drew his sword, shouting, "And who dies now?" the Pied Piper would draw himself up to his full height and boom magnificently, " *I!* said the Demon."

And at this moment, in the playground, the Pied Piper drew himself up to his full height, and although his voice was inaudible to Max, the detective smiled as he envisioned the sound of the magnificent delivery of the immortal four words and then saw the children jump and clap their hands with glee.

"I like him," Sylvia had said to Max, "because he's a darling old man and he's doing my groundwork. One of these days I'm going to have to cope with those kids in a classroom, and he's sending them to me prepared."

Sylvia loved short cuts.

Max loved Sylvia.

Would he ever be able to tell her? Would he ever again be able to commit himself fully to another human being? There had been his unloved wife and unloved son so cruelly immolated in a car crash and explosion. There had been occasional affairs of unloving unimportance, and then along came Sylvia Plotkin to help find her missing teen-aged student and . . . and write a damn book about it when he was trying to write the same damn book!

Damn you, Sylvia Plotkin! Damn your love, your kindness, your charity, your damn homemade chicken soup, which I loathe and one of these days I'll tell you so, and damn those dimples, which make your face look like an innocent child when you laugh, which is so damn often.

Max's face softened as he stared vacantly at the blank sheet of paper in the typewriter.

Sylvia Plotkin. Authoress. Best seller. Divorcee. Isaac Plotkin wherever you are do you writhe with jealousy and inner torment when Sylvia's name comes leaping out at you from an ad in the book sections?

I do.

Max sat up abruptly.

There! I've admitted it to myself. I envy Sylvia. That's why I started writing articles. That's why I started the book on Tippy. That's why I'm on edge and nervous and have no appetite and can't find an opening sentence for this Judge Kramer article. How many weeks did it take Melville to hit on "Call me Ishmael."

The intercom buzzed. Max flicked a switch and heard a visitor announced, Burton Lockwood of the San Francisco Police Department.

Edna St. Thomas Shelley lit her fifth cigarette in twenty minutes with the glowing stub of the fourth. Chloe Grace spooned her ninth glob of banana split, leaving the maraschino cherry for the last. Sylvia Plotkin dabbed her eyes and blew her nose in a tissue, which she crumpled into a ball and deposited into the ashtray.

"Have a sip of coffee," E.S.T. suggested to Sylvia.

Sylvia shook her head no as her eyes began misting again. "The embarrassment," she said in a choked voice. "Plotkin in tears on a major network. And that producer trying to tell me it's human interest! Tears are personal and private and should never be exploited, don't you agree, Chloe?"

Chloe *tsk*'d and clucked her tongue for good measure and resumed spooning.

Edna blew a smoke ring that missed Chloe's head by half an inch and collided with one of Schrafft's tidier waitresses. "Those tears'll sell another ten thousand copies at the least."

"But supposing *Max* sees the program! He's sometimes at home during prime time."

Edna shrugged. "So he'll feel like a heel."

"Are we talking about the same Max?"

Chloe swallowed the maraschino cherry, dabbed daintily at her thin lips with her even thinner napkin and then folded her hands on the table. "Wait till Ramona sees the show. She never misses it. Will I get what for." She now favored Edna. "Up until this past July my sister and I were recluses for over thirty years. You know," she added matter-of-factly, "like the Collier Brothers. We never really did it deliberately. It just surrounded us and stuck. Then Sylvia and the Pied Piper broke the sound barrier."

"I hope he ate something hot today," said Sylvia mournfully.

"The Pied Piper?"

"Max."

E.S.T.'s fist connected with the table, the crockery clattered, Chloe shrunk into her chair and Sylvia stared around in embarrassment.

"Never in my life," raged Edna, "never in my life have I

heard such a carry-on about a mere man!"

Sylvia leaned forward and shot each word like a poisoned dart. "There aren't that many available, Edna." She trilled "Edna."

"Neither is this one!" said Edna after a sledgehammer snort. Then she clenched her fist and positioned it under Sylvia's chin. "Within your grasp you have fame and fortune, and you're ready to throw it to the winds for this egotistical, self-centered, single-minded . . ."

". . . doll."

"Fame and fortune isn't everything." Chloe spoke with a gentleness that always demanded respect and attention. "Ramona and I had it once, and all it brought us was loneliness. Looking back on it, I suppose we were very silly, very giddy young girls. We thought there'd be something better driving up in the next Rolls Royce, so we . . . left the men we had and" —she looked up with a forced smile—"and settled for dust and ashes."

Edna's eyes narrowed as only an editor's eyes can when she knows a sequence needs rewriting. "Thirty or so years ago you were still young and beautiful and, I assume, clever . . ."

"Oh, *terribly* clever." The edge in Chloe's voice didn't escape Sylvia.

"Then it wasn't men that made you shut yourselves away from the world," Edna stated with the authority of a specialist informing a patient she was a terminal case.

"My dear girl," said Chloe softly, "how little you know of life." Edna's jaw dropped, and Sylvia knew she would treasure the moment forever. Chloe aimed her mouth at Sylvia. "Take it from an old campaigner, sweetheart. You got yourself a leading man. Stick with him through the third act and the notices might be in your favor. Let me tell you, if I had my life to live over again, I wouldn't. Now to face Ramona. What's my share of the check?"

"It's on me."

Sylvia knew Edna wasn't just treating, she was passing sentence.

"But then," Chloe added cryptically, "it's never too late to make amends, is it? To one's self, that is." She patted her hennaed hair, pushed her chair away from the table and left.

Edna incinerated her sixth cigarette. "There goes another book." Sylvia waited. "Chloe and Ramona." Sylvia's mouth formed an O. "Why do two pretty hustlers suddenly take a powder on the world? Who were their men? What kind of bums were they? What was their era? Late twenties? Early thirties?" Smoke emanated from her nostrils like an angry bull. "Easy. Gangsters. Racketeers. Start digging, Sylvia, you might come up with some interesting corpses."

"Really, Edna, you're outrageous. They're just two dear old darlings who lost touch with reality. Why, if my Pied Piper hadn't barged in on them and jollied them back into the world . . . why . . . why . . . they'd still be rotting away."

"You're sure they were just rotting? Not . . . waiting?"

"For what, for crying out loud!"

"Search me. Editors don't research for their authors. And there's a book there someplace. I know. I can smell it. Now about this Van Larsen nonsense . . ."

It was unusual for Max Van Larsen to like a person on sight, but that's how the San Francisco detective affected him. Burton Lockwood was in his early fifties and reluctantly going to paunch. He had a wide-open face with a mouth to match, and wasted no time about getting down to business. He smoked large cigars, yet with this man Max didn't find it offensive. His friendly smile as he entered the office, his firm handshake, the way he took command of the chair offered him, the swiftness with which he unzipped his briefcase, extracted a photograph and placed it on the desk in front of Max—it all added up to the kind of professional attitude Max appreciated and too infrequently encountered. There was even the pride in which he clipped "Burton Lockwood, Parole Officer, San Francisco" with an air of confidence that made Max recognize him as a blood brother.

Max studied the photograph carefully. He saw an oval face with a lantern law, a jagged scar that ran from left ear to mouth, a snubbed nose and an egg-bald head. Only the eyes looked good. They were alert, alive and mocking.

"Who is he?" asked Max.

That was when Lockwood lit the cigar. "Roscoe Mears." He waited for a reaction and got a totally unexpected one, a Gallic shrug. "Means nothing to you?"

"Never saw the face before."

"Maybe you saw this one." Lockwood extracted another photograph from his briefcase and placed it in front of Max. It was yellowed at the edges and cracked, but not so the face it displayed. Here was a handsome dandy with twinkling eyes, a full head of wavy hair, face unscarred, but the lantern jaw and snubbed nose unmistakable.

"That's the 'before,' " said Lockwood with a smile. "It was taken thirty-six years ago." Max was still perplexed. "If you knew your vaudeville, you'd know Roscoe Mears." Max settled back and waited. "Roscoe was a singer and a raconteur. He was a top act for some six or seven years. But he had bigger ambitions." Max nodded encouragement. "He wanted a night club of his own in New York, and in nineteen thirty he got it. He wanted to be a star in the movies, and in nineteen thirty-one he got that. One picture made here in New York with a lot of the top local talent. It bombed but it still shows up on television from time to time."

"How'd he graduate to San Quentin?"

"Gradually. He was in a show on Broadway in twenty-nine and met some friends." He flicked some ash in a tray and then continued. "Among them, numerous powerful gangsters"—Max sat up—"and Judge Mathew Kramer. *Armand* Mathew, to give him full credit. The cigar bothering you?"

Max wondered what color his face had turned to exact that concern. "Not at all," he said, "but I happen to have a commission to do an article on the missing Kramer for *True Mystery Magazine.*"

"Well, what do you know!" said Lockwood, his face lighting up. "I happen to do a little writing of my own on the side." He patted his briefcase. "Hoping to kill two birds with one stone in New York. Just finished a book." He spoke the title with reverence. *"Parole Officer.* I was going to call it *Lockwood's Concern* but some creep named John O'Hara beat me to it."

Max valiantly battled the cascade of laughter attempting to gush its way out of his mouth. Sylvia Plotkin, how you'd love this moment.

"Anyway," said Lockwood, "let's join hands and continue singing with Roscoe. So you're doing an article on Kramer . . . Well, I may be a godsend instead of a nuisance. You see"—he leaned forward—"a lot of us think Roscoe knows where the body's buried."

"When did Mears jump his parole?"

"Little over a year ago. He'd been out three months."

"If Mears was so hot, why'd they let him out?"

"Oh, we were more than anxious to extend his lease, but the parole board overruled us. There was a smart shamus working for Mears."

Lockwood mentioned a name that had cropped up occasionally in Van Larsen's research on the missing Judge Kramer.

Said Van Larsen, "He used to be a so-called clerk for Morgan Montescue."

Lockwood nodded as Max referred to the notes on his legal pad. "I have Montescue listed among the missing," said Max.

"Revise it. He's still around. Here in New York."

"You're so sure?"

"I have no exact address or zone number, but I'm sure. We think he's one of the old associates Roscoe Mears is looking for, and I'll explain that in depth. Just listen closely, and if you get lost, just give a yell and I'll elucidate further."

There was no need for Max to either yell or seek deeper elucidation. Lockwood's narrative was clear and to the point and it completely absorbed Max's attention.

Lockwood told Max that when Mears was released from San Quentin, the shamus met him and staked him. The shamus, Lockwood added significantly, had a reputation for not wasting time, money or effort on small pickings. Therefore, it was Lockwood's suspicion that Mears' release might have been ordered by the mysterious Morgan Montescue.

"Look at it this way," said Lockwood, "Mears and the shamus are both linked to Montescue. Montescue and Mears were linked to Judge Kramer. The judge disappears with a quarter of a million bucks. You with me?"

Max nodded.

Lockwood continued. "Somewhere in that intimate little circle there's the possible answer where Kramer disappeared to. Now something tells me that here, in New York, the circle widens and the cast of characters increases. There's Kramer's widow, Lita Swenson."

"She's around," said Max.

Lockwood was ahead of Van Larsen. "According to my most recent tracer she's living in one of Judge Kramer's houses out in Brooklyn on Ocean Parkway." He stroked his chin for a moment. "She wasn't much help to the police when her husband vanished. According to my research she sang two performances of *Carmen* on Staten Island, cracked during the 'Habanera' and checked into a rest home for three years with a case of amnesia. A very expensive rest home, I might add.

"Kramer," he continued, "did a lot of dabbling in real estate. Lita still gets a very tidy income from his holdings." He sat back in his chair and then gently tugged at his left earlobe. "Now we come to the lady known as Nola Kemp . . ."

Max interrupted. "I've been trying to get a line on her for two months, but no luck."

"Join the club. But she's alive."

"You're so sure?"

"Very."

"Why?"

Lockwood leaned forward and explained. The San Francisco shamus put a tail on Mears immediately following his release from prison. The tail in question was a private investigator of dubious ethics and a frequent police informer. Mears was soon wise to the situation but kept his cool until he was ready to make his break from San Francisco. Mears rid himself of the tail by luring him to a shady section of the city, where the private investigator was beaten to a near-pulp by hired thugs.

"When he regained consciousness several days later," said Lockwood with a knowing wink of the eye, "he was most co-operative. He implied Mears was coming to New York to murder somebody."

"Well, certainly not Montescue," insisted Max. "If he's as shrewd as the legends say he is, he wouldn't help spring his potential killer."

"If he's as shrewd as the legends say he is," repeated Lockwood.

Max thought a moment, then looked at Lockwood quizzically. "Lita?"

Lockwood looked noncommittal.

Max spoke a third name. "Nola Kemp."

Lockwood smiled. "I knew you'd pick up my radar. Nola's a dark horse but my money's on her nose. She was Kramer's mistress, and the mistress always knows more than the wife or the lawyer. If she didn't know so much and was therefore so frightened, she wouldn't have kept herself hidden all these years. You see, Nola was always a bit of a mystery."

Nola Kemp had never been seen in public with Judge Kramer. In fact, Lockwood's thorough investigation into Nola Kemp's habits proved her to be a thorough recluse. Kramer had provided her with a secret love nest and she apparently kept to it. Even Kramer's wife, Lita, was unaware of Nola Kemp's existence. Lita was concentrating heavily on becoming an opera star, and to keep her concentration undivided, Kramer had financed Ezio Puccini's opera company to star her.

"Kramer seems to have been unusually wealthy," said Max.

Lockwood crossed his legs with an effort. "Too unusually wealthy. He was due for an income-tax rap at the time he disappeared. Had the Feds grabbed him, it might have opened up too many cans of peas . . . or garbage pails . . . depending on your choice of allusions."

"Then Kramer could have been ordered killed."

"He could have, and he might have been tipped and so took a long trip into thin air. Now, once Judge Kramer disappeared, there's not a further line on Nola Kemp. She's somewhere out there in thin air too." He uncrossed his legs with the assistance of his right hand. "But once we find Morgan Montescue, I think we'll find he has a direct line to her." Max leaned forward with increasing interest. "Morgan Montescue has a dummy corporation that's been paying real estate taxes on some Greenwich Village property in the name of Nola Kemp."

Max exhaled loudly. "And I have the *chutzpah* to attempt an article on Kramer without even a line of this."

Lockwood shrugged, and then spoke sympathetically. "It was the same with Shakespeare and *Richard the Third*. Anyway, I'm here to bring your facts up to date, and you'll help me find Mears. Am I right in thinking we can work well together?"

"Dead right," replied Max, and Lockwood subdued an urge to bear-hug him. "Question . . . if you can trace a dummy corporation owned by Montescue, why can't you trace Montescue?"

"The corporation is administered by a very reliable, venerable and trusted firm of attorneys who stick to the letter of the law where privileged information is concerned. They've been checked thoroughly and they're absolutely clean. When and if it's necessary, I'll pressure the one person who can probably lead us to Montescue."

"The San Francisco shamus," said Max.

"Right!" said Lockwood, slapping his knee. "We're beautiful together. Ever try writing a book?"

Max almost blanched.

"Great discipline. You ought to write a book. Now let's get back to Nola. I'm positive Mears knew her. Whether he's found her or not is another story. I think he hasn't because she hasn't turned up dead."

"You're that sure he intends to kill her?"

"He may not intend to, but he may have to. It's like I said, I think Nola knows too many answers. Why and how Judge Kramer disappeared . . . what happened to the money . . . and a few other odds and ends that could use tidying up."

"Why did Mears go to jail?"

"I think he was framed."

Max crossed to the electric percolator and plugged it into the outlet. "Why and by whom?"

Lockwood took Max back thirty-five years. Roscoe Mears had suffered two financial setbacks. His night club folded and his film flopped. Mob money was involved, the investments having undoubtedly been made through Judge Kramer. As far as the mob was concerned, Roscoe was permitted to pay back the losses, not with cash but by fronting a bootlegging operation in San Francisco. The setup there was so arranged that if the Feds ever closed in, Roscoe would take the rap. The Feds closed in and Roscoe ended up in San Quentin.

The coffee was now poured and the two detectives sat facing each other again.

"I think Mears was glad to take the rap," said Lockwood, to Max's surprise. "He knew too much about the mob's operation and probably too much about Kramer's disappearance. He'd be safer in cold storage. You wouldn't happen to have any Sweeta, would you?"

Max reached into the center drawer of his desk and complied with Lockwood's request.

"Of course, Roscoe didn't expect to get lumbered with a life sentence." Lockwood chuckled as he stirred the coffee. "How mischievous the Fates. See that scar crossing from his ear to his mouth? He got that in Quentin. He was attacked in the showers by a small-time spiv, on orders, we suspect, from the boys on top. The spiv got shoved before he could talk, but Roscoe has something to remember him by." He sipped his coffee. "Excellent."

Max was letting his coffee cool. "So Roscoe comes to New York to find Nola and the money and will murder to get it if necessary. There's something missing, Burton. I have a feeling there's another motive running parallel to Nola and the Kramer fortune."

Lockwood lowered his cup and smacked his lips. "You're beautiful, Van Larsen. Beautiful. I think there *is* someone else Roscoe is anxious to get to." Lockwood relished the interest in Van Larsen's face. "A girl friend."

"After *thirty-five* years?"

Lockwood found Max's naïveté charming. "Well, what the hell, didn't Evangeline finally get hers after some three decades?"

(And how many decades will *you* have to wait, Sylvia Plotkin?)

"So here I am," said Lockwood with a contented grin, "in the big city at last, with an assignment, a manuscript, and a very cooperative New York City police force."

"Who do you suggest we begin with? Lily? Puccini? The hunt for Montescue?"

"Noooo," said Lockwood, rubbing his chin, "there's another lead I'd like to consider. One of Nola's properties is an old reconverted church near Catherine Slip."

Max stared at the man.

"You know the one I mean?"

"I know it well. It's considered a landmark. Slightly ruined now, but still beautiful—complete with small graveyard and bell tower. It was reconverted into a residence some forty years ago."

"Right—but never occupied until late in nineteen thirty-two, and according to my information, still occupied by the original tenants."

"Yes," said Max.

"You know them? I think they may have known Kramer and very probably Nola Kemp."

"I know them," said Max, "they're sisters. Chloe and Ramona Grace."

C H A P T E R **III**

Gypsy Marie Rachmaninoff stood in front of her ground-floor establishment on Seventh Avenue and stared with a practiced and knowing eye at the passing scene, which was obviously not in the mood to have its future foretold. Between her teeth she clenched a corncob pipe. Her head was swathed in a paisley turban fringed with imitation pearls. Her puffed-sleeve blouse and voluminous skirt, which reached her ankles, were a Technicolor dream of rich purple and orange polka dots (blouse) and yellow, green and puce nymphs and satyrs (skirt). Around her shoulders was loosely draped a fading cotton shawl embossed with the signs of the zodiac.

The window of her store was heavily draped. On the glass was painted a crystal ball over which was lettered:

GYPSY MARIE
sees all! knows all! tells much!
Cards and tea leaves a
specialty!
COME INSIDE

"I am the long-lost daughter of a Tatar prince," she once told Sylvia Plotkin over steaming hot toddies, "and my mother was an Iranian duchess." Sylvia wasn't sure they had duchesses in Iran, but she never challenged the always-diverting Gypsy Marie. As to her long-departed husband, Gypsy Marie commented darkly and acidly, "He was last seen clinging to the spire of the Empire State Building swatting airplanes."

The seeress shivered against the October cold as she drew the shawl tighter around her shoulders. There were rarely clients on weekdays. Only the weekend tourists could be relied upon for enough money to pay for rent, food and possibly a new pair of shoes for her son. An oil stove provided added heat to the single but sizable room in the back of the store that passed for living quarters.

Gypsy Marie removed the pipe from her teeth and in a seductively husky voice shouted, "The future! Let me tell you the future! Gypsy Marie is infallible! Come inside and for one dollar I will tell you the future!"

"The bomb!" cried a woman with short-cropped hair, wearing puttees and a trench coat and slapping a riding crop against leather boots. "That's the future, baby, the bomb!"

"But after the bomb?" yodeled Gypsy Marie, who could rarely be topped.

"I need you," said the plaintive voice at Gypsy Marie's left elbow. The fortuneteller turned and gazed into a pair of Dostoevsky-sad eyes.

"Indeed, Sylvia Plotkin? Come inside and we shall plumb the depths of my crystal ball."

Two minutes later Sylvia stared anxiously at the turbaned head peering almost hypnotically into the white globe that rested on a metal base. Then, slowly, Gypsy Marie raised her head, and stared at a point fifteen degrees over Sylvia's head and passed her hands slowly over the ball.

"The ball is cold," she explained to the ceiling.

Sylvia bit her lip.

Gypsy Marie closed her eyes, continued passing her hands

over the ball and began chanting:

> "Kabala, Kabala, Kabala, Kabala,
> Gods of the darkness, hear my call,
> This is Gypsy Marie Rachmaninoff,
> Clear my crystal ball."

Her eyes flew open, her head snapped down as she placed her hands flat on the table. "You are deeply troubled."

Sylvia opened her purse and pulled out a tissue.

"A man."

Sylvia nodded and dabbed at her nose, sniffling intermittently.

"Van Larsen?"

"Well, of course it's Van Larsen! You've seen us together often enough!"

"Who's reading this ball?"

"Sorry."

Gypsy Marie passed her hands over the ball as she glared at Sylvia. "You've annoyed the ball. I am getting very poor reception."

Sylvia wondered if there were special antennas for crystal balls. She even felt like a superstitious fool for continually patronizing the fortuneteller, but Gypsy Marie *had* predicted her book would be published and would get excellent notices, including Eliot Fremont-Smith—and so what if he didn't review it. That other one in the *Times* raved, and that was close enough for Sylvia.

"The ball is clearing." With one end of her shawl she began wiping the ball vigorously. "Damn flies." Then she cleared her throat and spoke slowly. "Van Larsen is jealous."

The tissue was back at the nose again.

"Your success has gone to his head."

Sylvia nodded sadly.

Gypsy Marie's voice brightened. "But he loves you!"

"He *does?*" squealed Sylvia with delight.

"Not very passionately, but then, for Van Larsen, a handshake is passion. Hmmmm."

"What? What? What is it?"

"I see a cloud.

"A nimbus?"

"A cloud is a cloud." Gypsy Marie glanced at Sylvia in exasperation. Teachers. *Pfah.* She returned to the ball. "It is a very dark cloud." Her voice trembled. "A dangerous cloud."

"He's in trouble!"

Gypsy Marie looked up slowly. "The cloud hangs over . . . *you!*"

Dumbstruck, Sylvia stared at the pointed finger. "Me?"

"It is a matter, my dear," said Gypsy Marie sweetly, "of minding your own business. However, let me look further. Perhaps beyond the cloud there is sunshine." Her eyes narrowed. "More clouds."

"Maybe it's the ball. Maybe it needs another wipe. Here, I have a clean tissue."

"The ball is clear!" snapped Gypsy Marie. "I see dark clouds, and when I see dark clouds they are for-real dark clouds!" She picked up her pipe from an ash tray and sucked on it. "These clouds began forming today. Possibly a few hours ago?"

"Well," said Sylvia, "I made a perfect idiot of myself on a TV show I taped this afternoon . . ."

"Go on."

"And then afterward, at Schrafft's, I had this argument with my editor, and of course there was a very strange scene with . . ."

"With . . . ?"

"With Chloe Grace."

"Ahhh? Indeed? I shall look further."

(*There's a book there someplace. I know. I can smell it.*)

Sylvia dabbed at a bead of perspiration on her forehead and couldn't understand what it was doing there, because the rest of her was shivering.

•   •   •

Jingle jangle jingle jangle.

The bells at the end of the pendant earrings were attached to the earlobes of a mountain of a woman, easily six feet tall, with two hundred extremely well distributed pounds, and jet-black hair pulled back tightly in a bun held in place by a Spanish comb. She wore black stretch pants, a man's shirt open at the neck and a tired mink jacket. The room across which she was pacing with a thumping tread was overfurnished and cold. Only her guest seemed bothered by the temperature as she warmed her hands on a glass of piping-hot tea.

She too was tall, easily as tall as Madame Vilna and equally buxom. What distinguished her from the other woman was a garish blue wig and a surgical mask across her face, which covered mouth and nose.

Madame Vilna, beef-trust legs planted firmly on the carpet, addressed the garish blue wig. "You must!" Her voice rang with the power of Big Ben.

"Like hell I will," came the other's gargled reply.

"It is impossible . . . absolutely impossible to give a performance in that . . . that"—pointing with trembling hand at the surgical mask—"cam-ou-flaaaaage!"

"Listen, Vilna, if I was an Eskimo I'd find your place enchanting. Can't you raise some steam?"

"Are you blind? I am boiling over!"

Madame Vilna thumped to the fireplace, picked up a log and flung it on the embers, and framed against a shower of sparks, crossed back to confront her guest. Her voice, when she spoke, was unexpectedly charming and softly modulated. Madame Vilna was an old practitioner at the element of surprise. "My dear Ramona, enchanting creature, bosom friend, if briefly. Several months ago, when due to the entreaties of two very lovable mortals you and your charming sister emerged from your *cen*-turies of self-imposed *see*-questration . . ."

". . . Chloe talked me into it . . ."

"*That* is neither here nor yonder. The fact is you are *out* and

you are *here"*—one finger pointing ominously at the floor—
"and at darling Sylvia Plotkin's suggestion, I have taken unto
you as my partner in my dramatic readings. Now then"—hands
on hips and head thrust forward like an inquisitive turtle emerging from its shell to get an idea of the weather—"how . . .
howwww . . . do we confront my audience at the Workmen's
Circle, me wearing Loehmann's and *you* a surgical mask! It
must *go!"*

"Never." Ramona Grace got to her feet and smoothed her
tweed skirt. "I should never have agreed to this nonsense."

"Nonsense! When Vilna *reads"*—finger pointing at the ceiling—"the earth trembles!"

"Then positively count me out. I'm shaky on my feet as it
is."

Very gently Madame Vilna extended a beefy hand, connected
with Ramona's bosom, and Ramona was back in the chair with
a look of astonishment. The hands were back on the hips again
as Madame Vilna gazed into Ramona's gray eyes. "My dear,"
she said softly, "what is behind the mask?"

"I told you before," said Ramona indignantly, "scars . . .
hideous, awful disgusting scars."

"I mean the *real* mask." The index finger almost connected
with Ramona's nose. *"You. Ramona."*

Ramona slapped the hand away. "You ask too many questions, baby."

"I suppose you never saw me as Pesha in *Ich Vill Mein
Phunt of Fleisch*. To you, Portia in *The Merchant of Venice.*"
Then, storming, the index finger once more aimed at the ceiling
and trembling, "That is what I am asking from you! The quality
of mercy! I have rehearsed you for weeks and at last you are
passable! You *must* remove the mask!"

Ramona screamed.

"I have perhaps offended you?"

"There's someone at the window!"

With the reflexes of an athlete in his prime, Madame Vilna

spun about, rushed to the glass double doors leading to the garden, flung the doors wide in one furious gesture and raced after the crouching figure scurrying toward the fence.

"Now I've got you!" shrieked Madame Vilna. "I have caught you at last!"

The crouching figure's pathetic attempt to scale the wall into the neighboring backyard was curtailed by a quintet of beefy fingers firmly gripping the collar of his threadbare jacket.

"Now," cried Madame Vilna, "retribution!"

Ramona Grace grabbed her purse and her coat and fled the apartment as Madame Vilna dragged the struggling hunch-backed boy back to the room. "Ramona? Ramona! Dear Moses! Why am I always abandoned in my hour of need!"

A cloudy twilight was beginning to settle over the playground as the Pied Piper reached the climax of the fairy tale *Rapunzel*. As he narrated, the children no longer saw a red-headed, red-bearded old man with patches of weatherbeaten face, they saw a handsome young prince with yellow hair, fair-skinned and im-passioned.

"Rapunzel, Rapunzel, let down your hair!"

The Pied Piper's voice was unusually soft and youthful, and the children sat variously—with chins cupped in hands, arms around each other or nervously rubbing ankles together—but thoroughly engrossed.

"And from the tower in which the beautiful Rapunzel was held prisoner by the wicked witch, there emerged from the turret window her beautiful face of infinite purity. She lowered her head and her lovely mile of flaxen hair wafted slowly to the ground. And then taking a firm grip on her hair, the prince began his dangerous climb to Rapunzel's rescue."

One freckled-faced youngster piped up, "It didn't hoit her?"

The Pied Piper smiled patiently. "It was magic hair."

The child was satisfied and recupped his chin.

"Slowly, slowly he climbed to the tower . . ."

As he spoke, the Pied Piper's eyes connected with two men emerging from the police precinct across the street. He recognized Max Van Larsen.

Lockwood nudged Van Larsen. "Who's the weird character hypnotizing those kids in the playground?"

"We call him the Pied Piper," said Max, and then briefly told him the story of the Pied Piper's descent on the neighborhood.

At the conclusion, Lockwood chortled. "He seems to have quite a way with those kids."

"He has quite a way with everyone. Let's go over. I'll introduce you. He's a bit of a character."

As they crossed the street to the playground, the Pied Piper spoke the final sentence of the story. "And so, children, they lived happily ever after!" His standing ovation would have brought a pang of envy to the bosom of a Broadway star.

"More!" cried the children, the freckled-faced boy shouting, "Aw come on, Pipe, tell us anudder!"

"Night is descending," said the Pied Piper fruitily, with a dramatic gesture toward the sky, "and it is time all youngsters were at home washing their hands and faces before dinner." Then, with a twinkle in his voice, "Now scat! Everybody home! Tomorrow at the same time!"

"The Demon story tomorrow, *please?*" begged an agitated nine-year-old.

"The Demon story it shall be," said the old man, and the children knew that behind the bushy red beard was a warm smile.

As the children began to disperse, the Pied Piper crossed toward Max and Lockwood.

"Piper," said Max, "I'd like you to meet a colleague of mine from San Francisco, Burton Lockwood."

"Delighted, Mr. Lockwood." He took the parole officer's hand and pumped it vigorously. "Is this your first visit to New York?"

"The first," replied Lockwood.

"Business or pleasure?"

Lockwood was inwardly amused at the mellifluous rise and fall of the old man's voice as the question undulated from his mouth.

"Strictly business, and the conclusion of it would bring me a great deal of pleasure."

"Ah," said the old man, "you sound very dark and very mysterious."

And you sound very theatrical and corny, Lockwood felt like saying, but instead told him the nature of his trip. Lockwood was a detective of the old school. He believed in .passing the word around, and with any luck, some word might get back to him.

Max was amused by the thin mockery in the old man's voice as he exclaimed with a dramatic flourish, "An escaped convict!"

"Not quite. Just a small-time parole jumper," Lockwood corrected.

The old man stroked his beard like a biblical patriarch. "Hardly small-time if you've traveled three thousand miles to reclaim him."

"Oh, he's small-time," said Lockwood, "but what I think he's about to get mixed up in is big-time."

The Pied Piper nodded thoughtfully. "One must never underestimate the probing mind, must one? Putting one's self in the mind of your parole jumper, he undoubtedly sees himself as insignificant and unimportant, unworthy of the expense of a concentrated pursuit. Yet here you are, Mr. Lockwood, playing Javert to his Jean Valjean."

Max restrained a wince.

"I wonder," continued the old man. "If your quarry knew the bloodhounds were at his rear and nipping, would he cower somewhere in fear, or revel in an inflated ego?"

"I should think a soupçon of both," suggested Max, soupçon annoyingly bringing to mind chicken soup and Sylvia Plotkin.

"We'd better get going," said Lockwood to Max. "Maybe

we'll be in time to join the ladies in a spot of tea."

"So delighted to have made your acquaintance," said the old man to Lockwood. "I'm sure we'll be running into each other again. Au revoir, Max." He turned and walked away from them toward the opposite end of the playground.

"Fruity old duck," commented Lockwood as he took Max's arm and led him to the street. "What's his background? His name?"

Max was suddenly chagrined to realize he had never probed into the old man's past—simply accepted him, as did everyone else, as a kindly, amusing, eccentric old duffer. Another anonymous Village character.

"You know, Burton," said Max with an embarrassed laugh, "it's never occurred to me to find out. Just another drifter, I guess."

Lockwood said, "He weaves an amazing spell over those kids."

"Over everyone," Max added, "I think he's finally found a home here."

Ramona Grace huddled in her coat against the icy gusts of October wind. One hand covered the surgical mask as she hurried down the street toward her home at the corner. The reconverted church stood in the center of an acre of land, surrounded by a high stone wall with an iron gate set in the middle of the wall. The gate opened onto a gravel path which was bordered on one side by trees and hedges tightly grown together in a horticultural maze. The other side of the path was an old graveyard that extended around to the rear of the church. The gravestones were old and worn and almost illegible. Church and graveyard dated back to the early seventeen-hundreds.

The building itself was a four-storied, near-crumbling Gothic nightmare from whose center rose an ominously imposing stone tower at the top of which hung a centuries-old cast-iron bell, beautifully embossed and fluted, with an old rope still attached.

Now the wind challenged the bell, and Ramona shivered as she always shivered when the clapper struck the sides and caused a ghostly, muffled reverberation.

She unlatched the gate, pushed it open and let it fall shut behind her as she hurried up the path. Through the closed shutters of one ground-floor window a reflection of electric light seeped through. She climbed ten stone steps, inserted a key in the lock of the door and entered.

"I'm in here!" she heard Chloe cry from the room that had once been the vestry. She didn't like the sound of Chloe's voice. "I have something terrible to tell you!"

She liked that less.

"Look at the boy!" cried Sylvia sympathetically. "He's absolutely quaking with fear!"

Sylvia's powers of observation could easily have been challenged. The boy wasn't quaking with fear at all. He was furiously attempting to escape the steel grip Madame Vilna had on his jacket collar. Gypsy Marie Rachmaninoff was a study in repose—her arms were folded and she was puffing benignly on the corncob pipe.

"Here!" cried Madame Vilna, still in a boiling rage as she shoved the boy toward his mother. "Here is your Peeping Tomashevsky!" Then sudden nostalgia caused a smile to wreathe her face. "You perhaps remember Boris Tomashevsky? I was once scheduled to co-star with him in *Dorten Dere Ligt Zie* which perhaps you might recall as *Desire Under the Elms,* but unfortunately, I was four months *enceinte* as they say in my native Rumania. Your boy," she suddenly stormed again, "is a *paskoodnyak!* He is a snoop! A nosy Parkinson! He is always looking in everybody's windows."

"He's curious," said Gypsy Marie sweetly as she put her arms around her son, her hand sliding easily and comfortably over the hump between his shoulders. The boy turned to Madame Vilna and made a face.

"Careful, sonny," said Madame Vilna, waving a threatening finger at him, "or your face will freeze like that."

"Apologize to Madame Vilna," said Gypsy Marie.

Silence.

"I said apologize!"

Silence.

"Quasimodo!"

The boy pulled away from her and leered at the former star of the Yiddish theater.

"Okay, okay!" he shouted. "Okay! Okay!" And he scurried into the living quarters behind the store.

Madame Vilna clasped her hands together and stared at the ceiling in supplication. "Dear God in heaven, why have you chosen to punish this fortuneteller and her poor deformed son? Her misfit . . ."

"He's not a misfit," snapped Gypsy Marie, "he's a changeling."

"Someday he will get into serious trouble."

"Who's the fortuneteller around here?" demanded Gypsy Marie.

"Quasimodo doesn't mean any harm, Madame Vilna," offered Sylvia. "He's a good boy."

Gypsy Marie sank into a chair and stared into space. "He's lonely. None of the kids will play with him. They laugh at him. They tease him." Softly, "They torture him." She looked up at Madame Vilna. "He looks in windows because he imagines himself a part of the people he's watching. He misses a real home and a real father and brothers and sisters. He doesn't like being a gypsy, even though his veins are laced with royal blood."

Madame Vilna winked at Sylvia as she addressed Gypsy

Marie. "Whose royal blood, darling?"

"Take your pick," said Gypsy Marie huskily and sadly. "I've had them all." She sucked on the pipe but the ember had died. She flung the pipe on the table, secured her chin with the palm of her left hand and crossed a leg. "You think I like this existence? I should be running a tea room, then I could furnish a decent place for the kid. Then maybe he'd take an interest in more important things."

"Like school," suggested Sylvia.

"He's no dummy," said Gypsy Marie. "He's a lot brighter than you think. Ask the Pied Piper. At least *he* talks to the kid. Quasi adores him." She emitted an ironic chuckle. "He calls him Grandpa. Someday"—she lifted her head proudly, displaying a magnificent Grecian profile—"someday, Piper says, everything my kid has absorbed with his eyes will manifest itself in a fantastic display of talent." She turned to Sylvia. "He can draw pretty good, you know."

"He most certainly can," agreed Sylvia, inwardly shuddering at the memory of some of his pornographic samples on the gymnasium walls. The things he must have seen through some windows! "If only," continued Sylvia, "if only he didn't have such a name. I mean, surely you must have been very bitter when you named him Quasimodo."

"I didn't name him that. The kids gave it to him when he was a little boy, and it stuck."

"How cruel. What's his real name?"

"Genghis."

"Oh. Pretty. Well, Madame Vilna? Going my way?"

"Your way is always my way, my dear. How did the television go today? I am looking forward to it with avidity. I have never been so eager since I was rehearsing *Vuss Fahr a Tsimmis Cuchts Du?* which might be more familiar to you as *Six Who Pass While the Lentils Boil.*"

"It went just dandy," said Sylvia in a flat voice. She turned to Gypsy Marie. "Why don't you and the boy come over later and watch the show with us? I've invited Madame Vilna, the Grace Sisters and the Pied Piper."

Gypsy Marie nodded her thanks.

Madame Vilna eyed Sylvia quizzically. "And we will not be enjoying Van Larsen's presence?"

"I think not," said Sylvia coldly. "Gypsy Marie did not see it in her crystal ball." She opened her purse, extracted several bills and pressed them into the fortuneteller's hand.

"It's too much," said Gypsy Marie.

"You undercharge," retorted Sylvia sharply, took Madame Vilna's hand and led her from the store.

"Quasi!" shouted Gypsy Marie. "Come in here, Quasi! I want to talk to you." There was no response. She got to her feet, muttering a few choice epithets under her breath, crossed to the back room, pushing aside the dividing bead curtains with one swoop, and stared at an open window. She rushed to the window, leaned out and shouted, "Quasi! Quasi! You haven't had your dinner, you silly kid!"

"I could kill you! I could absolutely kill you!"

"Cool it," snarled Chloe, "just cool it!"

She sat in an overstuffed easy chair, filing her nails. Ramona towered over her with fists clenched, the surgical mask removed, the series of hideous patchwork scars that covered her mouth, chin, nose and cheeks emphasizing evilly her hideous rage. The blue wig trembled like a dustball in the wake of a vengeful broom.

"I have myself to blame for all this!" cried Ramona as she moved away from Chloe and, wringing her hands, began pacing the room.

"Indeed you do," said Chloe coolly.

Ramona stopped in her tracks, turned slowly and stared at her sister. "You know something. I don't give a damn any longer."

Chloe looked up slowly, her eyes narrowing into grotesque

slits. "*You* don't give a damn. Thirty-six years in this filthy, miserable, stinking prison and *you* don't give a damn!" This was followed by a windup, a pitch—and the nail file missed by half an inch adding another mark on Ramona's disfigured face. Chloe leaped to her feet. "I enjoyed doing that show, you hear me? I enjoyed it! And I don't care *who* recognizes me and starts reviving the Kramer hullabaloo. There's a thing called statute of limitations, you ever hear of it?"

"You damn well know I have."

"We can't be touched now. Not by anyone. Not any more. We sentenced ourselves. We paid. I'll put the kettle on. Sylvia's expecting us at eight."

"I'm not going."

"Why not?"

"I'm never leaving this house again."

Chloe folded her arms and tapped a foot. "I see. You've had a taste of the rebirth and it's given you an upset stomach."

"I'm never leaving this house again!" shrieked Ramona. "I'm an old lady. A big, hideously disfigured old lady! Oh God, have we paid! Oh God, God, God, have I paid." Bitter tears fell in torrents and she covered her face with her hands.

Chloe spoke when the tears began to subside. "We could leave. We could leave tonight. We could go to Mexico, further if you like, where we're not known. We could try to make something of what's left of our lives."

Ramona uncovered her face, which now held a set expression. "You can go if you like. I'm staying here."

Chloe smiled. "How generous of you, Ramona. After thirty-six years, how generous. And what will you extend? A small settlement? A monthly allowance? An insulting fraction?"

"It's my money."

"Yes, dear, it is in theory your money. It is in your name. But by rights," she cried, "and you damn well know it, half of it's mine!"

It was Ramona's turn to smile. "I've been sharing it with you, haven't I?"

"You rotten bitch. I've a mind to give Van Larsen all the facts he needs."

Ramona shrugged. "I don't care any more. I've got nothing left. No reason to go on. I made a stab at it. I let you . . . and Plotkin . . . and"—she laughed almost melodiously—"that idiot *Pied Piper* talk me into facing the world again. Well, I faced it. I now choose to turn my back on it again. You can go on as you like. You want to leave? Leave. I'm staying here. It's all the world I want. I was happy here once. I can be happy here again, in my own way, with myself."

"Perhaps you're right," said Chloe. "Perhaps you deserve to spend the rest of your days here. Where's the money?"

Ramona sat in a chair and laughed.

"Where is it? You can tell me now. What difference does it make?"

"Thirty-six years, sweetheart, and you still haven't found it. Don't you think I've sat up nights listening to you scavenging in the tower rooms, in the cellar, in the kitchen? No, Chloe darling. As long as *I* and only *I* know where the money is, we are both safe." Her mood darkened. "Everything was fine, just fine, until we let *them* in. The second big mistake of my life." Slowly her fingers went to her face. "You should never have done this to me, Chloe."

The crouching hunchbacked figure loped along the street toward Robert Wagner High School, oblivious of the biting wind tearing at his threadbare clothes, aware only of the tears streaming down his face.

"Okay okay okay," he whispered to himself, "okay okay okay. Royal blood. Ha. Changeling—whatever the hell that is —ha. I'm a bastard. I know. I looked it up. Fortuneteller. Ha. I'll go away. I'll join a circus. With the freaks. Where I belong. I'll be a good freak. I'll swing on a trapeze. Okay okay okay. I'm the best in gym. On the bars. On the handrails. I'm the best. I'm a real swinger. Okay okay okay. I swung from the basketball hoop and the kids cheered. First time they cheered. Last time too. Quasimodo. Hunchback. Smart. Real smart. Pied Piper. He'll help me. My grandpa. Good guy. Real good guy. He's okay okay okay."

Lockwood's first reaction to the reconverted church was typical: "What an ugly heap." Then, once inside the gate, surrounded by hedges, trees and graveyard, he commented briskly, "But it certainly has character. Good location. Wonder if anyone's tried to buy it."

"Everyone," said Max. "But the ladies are fighters. They've got the Historical Society behind them. They're trying to have it designated an official city landmark, and they just might win."

The wind struck the bell and the reverberation caused Lockwood to gulp. "Weird," he said in a half-whisper, "real weird."

"I'd better prepare you for Ramona Grace," said Max as they trudged along the path. "She covers most of her face with a surgical mask, so spare her any embarrassing reaction."

"Trench mouth?" asked Lockwood blandly.

"Scars, or so a . . . uh . . . friend of mine was told."

From inside the house came a piercing scream. They took the steps two at a time and Max grasped the gargoyle knocker and pounded it rapidly.

Chloe rubbed her cheek as the pounding of the knocker echoed through the room. "You'll answer for this," she whispered to Ramona. "Just you wait. You'll answer for this."

Ramona's eyes never left Chloe as she reached for the surgical mask and firmly set it in place. "We have visitors, dear," she said sweetly, "invaders from the outside world. Be a good little bunny and put the kettle on." Arms held stiffly at her side, she went to open the door.

Max was reaching for the knocker again when the door opened. Max didn't bother with amenities. "Was that you who screamed?"

"No, Max, it was Chloe. She thought she saw a mouse." She turned to Lockwood, and her eyes traveled to his briefcase. "Selling tickets to the policemen's ball?"

Max introduced Lockwood and stated the reason for the visit.

"Nola Kemp," said Ramona in a half-whisper. "I haven't heard the name in years. Come in. You're just in time for tea."

Lockwood nudged Max and they followed Ramona into the vestry.

In the kitchen Chloe held a sharp knife in her hand. Viciously she plunged it into a chocolate cake and began slicing, muttering oaths and imprecations under her breath. The kettle whistled, and she grabbed a dishcloth and moved the kettle from stove to table, pouring hot water into the tea jug in which several spoonfuls of tea waited to be inundated.

And then, from the corner of her eye, she saw the face at the window.

"Nola Kemp," said Ramona, "was quite a stunner in her day." She sat in an easy chair near the fireplace, facing the two detectives on the sofa, a coffee table forming an island between them. "She only appeared in the one show. In twenty-nine, I think it was."

"Nineteen thirty-one," Lockwood corrected her.

Ramona shrugged. "She did what we called a flash act. It was all she did. Just those two minutes. A Javanese dancing act, wearing little more than a temple mask. Nobody ever saw her arrive at the theater. Nobody ever saw her leave. She was quite a mystery to all of us. It made for very good publicity for the show, and for a short time, for Nola. She disappeared after that."

"But you managed to become her friend." It was Lockwood who spoke.

"Whatever makes you think that?"

"This property is in her name."

Ramona interlaced her fingers. "Oh yes. The registration is a bit misleading, as I assume that's where you got your information. Actually, this house was bought in Nola's name by her friend Judge Kramer."

Max lit a cigarette and Lockwood asked Ramona if she minded a cigar.

"The judge always smoked cigars," she said. "I'm one of the few women who adores the aroma. Go right ahead."

"Then this house," said Max, "belongs to Judge Kramer's widow?"

"This house is mine."

Max pursed his lips for a moment, then spoke. "Why didn't you have the registration transferred?"

"It was," said Ramona with a smile, "by my attorney. Since Nola disappeared without a trace, and in order to preserve mine and my sister's anonymity, we requested and received permission to retain Nola's name on the registration. I have all the necessary proof of ownership."

"Your attorney wouldn't be Morgan Montescue?"

Ramona turned to Lockwood and answered his question. "He was then. I no longer retain one. There's been no need."

Max asked, "Where is Montescue these days?"

"Dead, I should think."

"He's quite alive," said Lockwood.

Ramona crossed a still-shapely leg. "I'm sure Max has told you, Mr. Lockwood, my sister and I have been out of touch for thirty-six years, until recently."

Chloe was entering with the tray of tea and cake.

Lockwood was asking, "Have you heard from Roscoe Mears lately?"

The tray slipped from Chloe's hands and crashed to the floor.

CHAPTER V

"Butterfingers!"

Ramona's voice broke the awkward silence that followed the crash. Chloe stepped back and stared at the mess at her feet. "I baked that cake myself," was all she could say. The spilled tea formed a large puddle between herself and the others.

"Let me help," said Max, rising and dodging one of Lockwood's smoke rings as he crossed to Chloe.

"Don't bother, Max," said Chloe, fighting to control her voice. "I'll clear it up."

"Oh, *I'll* do it," said Ramona testily. "Chloe always makes such a mess of things."

Chloe's eyes met her sister's briefly, and Max knew that had he stepped between them, he would have been electrocuted. Chloe stepped around the puddle past Max and sat down next to Lockwood. She introduced herself, and Lockwood made a feeble attempt at a joke as Max helped Ramona pile the debris onto the tray.

"It was your mentioning Roscoe Mears," said Ramona with

an effort as she straightened up, eying the puddle with distaste. "Roscoe always had a strange effect on Chloe. Roscoe used to be sweet on Chloe."

"A lot of Johns were sweet on Chloe," said Chloe in a voice that could have cut through oak.

Max was holding the tray and wondering if it was up to him to take it to the kitchen. He didn't know where the kitchen was. Ramona might have been reading his mind. "I'll take it," she said. She had a firm grip on the tray before Max could politely remonstrate, and left the room as Lockwood began questioning Chloe.

"Has Roscoe tried to get in touch with you recently?" he asked.

Chloe was dabbing at the hem of her dress with a handkerchief. "No." She wet the handkerchief with her tongue and attacked a spot of chocolate.

Lockwood shifted for a better view of her. Her garish hair and make-up offended his eye. For all his outward bluster, he was a man who favored subtlety and moderation.

Chloe was speaking again. "Why should he want to get in touch with me?"

"You're an old friend," said Lockwood softly, "and there are probably very few of those left."

Chloe abandoned the skirt, tucked the handkerchief into her sleeve, folded her hands and looked almost demure. "Mr. Lockwood, if Roscoe's on the lam, I doubt he'd try to contact anyone. As I recall"—she stared at the ceiling dreamily—"he was never one given to trust or confidences. In my day Roscoe was what we used to call a lone wolf."

"But if he was sweet on you . . ."

"There's sweet," she interrupted rudely, "and there's *sweet*. I was busy elsewhere." Max was now sitting opposite them. "I was mostly Rightie's girl." The statement came at them like the hostile palm of a hand. "In those days, if you had to be somebody's girl, you chose the biggest. The best was never available.

I liked Rightie. Believe it or not, in private, away from everyone else, he was very sweet and very tender, a real gent. He was good to me and that's all that mattered."

There was a loud crash from the kitchen, and Max jumped to his feet.

"Sit down, Max," said Chloe calmly. "She's just having one of her snits. That was the good tea set I wrecked."

"Sounded like something falling over," said Max.

"I'll give you odds you hear something else in a few minutes. Ramona's anger gives vent in cycles."

There was another crash, and Max made a move toward the hall.

"Sit down, Max!" cried Chloe, this time sharply. "She'll be over it in a minute and be back in here as sweet as pie. I've lived with this jazz for thirty-six years. I know all the cues. I'm supposed to come running to her and make sympathetic noises. Well, I'm not, so just relax and sit it out." Max sat reluctantly. Chloe smiled. "We were going at each other when you two got here. You probably heard me scream. She belted me one." She was as matter-of-fact as a pickpocket in a crowded subway. "You look shocked, Max. Don't be so naïve. Two women cooped up together like this. What'd you expect?" She removed the handkerchief from her sleeve and wiped the corners of her mouth. "We never thought this would happen to us." Her hand swept the room and then dropped into her lap. "The years just accumulated. We didn't even notice each other growing old." She sighed. "We were always devoted. We were orphaned when we were kids." A defiant look crossed her face. "It was us against the world, and it was one hell of a battle. We weren't smart then. Just pretty. Pretty was our only asset so we invested it and it paid dividends. The Sisters Grace!" She spoke with pride and her eyes were sparkling. "Not the Grace Sisters. The *Sisters* Grace. It had class. That's how we were billed. No talent, just looks. But we weren't giddy like most of the other flips. We saw to it we'd have umbrellas for our rainy days. That is"—she paused for a moment and looked toward the hall—"Ramona saw to it." Her eyes found Max. "Ramona was the brains of the organization. Why'd you think Roscoe would look us up?"

She took both men by surprise. Lockwood removed the cigar from his mouth, crossed his legs, cleared his throat, then filled her in.

She said thoughtfully, "So Morgan helped spring Roscoe." She shook her head sadly. "Why don't they let well enough alone. It's the Kramer money they're after, you know, and God knows where that is."

"And Nola Kemp," added Lockwood.

"Smarter boys have tried to find Nola. Let me give you a tip, gentlemen." She leaned forward conspiratorially. "Nola appeared from out of nowhere and went right back there when Armand Kramer disappeared. No one will ever find her. And if I know Roscoe, you won't find him either."

"You're so sure." This was Max, and very annoyed. He heard mockery and saw challenge and felt blood rushing to his face.

"Keep your cool, Max," said Chloe evenly. "I speak from experience, and there is nothing so eloquent as experience. They never found Kramer, did they? They'll never find Nola. As for Roscoe, fifty gets you five hundred he's no longer in the country."

"He had very little money," said Lockwood, carefully studying the parched face.

"Fifty gets you five hundred," she repeated.

Max suddenly wondered why Ramona hadn't rejoined them. "Shouldn't you look in on Ramona?"

"She'll be out when she's ready. Probably waiting for the kettle to boil. Ramona's a pot watcher. She's had years of practice."

Lockwood sighed. "You can't help us with Nola or Roscoe. How about Morgan Montescue? Any idea where he might be?"

"In hell, with any luck. I loathed him. Still loathe him. Will always loathe him."

"Very generous of so loathsome a man to help spring Roscoe," said Lockwood.

"I don't know what any of that's about." She was blunt and firm. "If there was anything between Roscoe and Morgan, Ramona and I weren't in on it. We knew Roscoe fronted for Rightie in that club and that movie." She paused as though listening for something, and then continued. "He fronted that deal in Frisco that got him sent up." Max had the feeling she was fighting back tears.

Suddenly she shouted to Max, "Why don't you make it up with Sylvia?" Max was dumfounded at the sudden transition. Lockwood looked perplexed. "She's the best you'll ever find, that's for sure!" She leaped to her feet, and with her hands folded behind her back, began pacing in a small circle. "What's wrong with you men anyway? Women do things they think are going to please you and all we get is a kick in the behind." She stopped in front of Max and stared down at him angrily. "She's pining away! She makes Camille look like Kate Smith! She burst into tears at the end of the program today!"

(The program! Max groaned to himself. Tonight. Sylvia. Network television. Authoress. Plotkin. Sylvia.)

"You look sick," snapped Chloe. "You deserve it. You both better go. Ramona won't be coming back. I can tell she's having a real bad one. She knows what I know and I've said all I have to say." She turned to Lockwood. "Maybe another time." She rocked on her heels and stared at the ceiling. "Maybe Ramona was right. We should have stayed behind these walls. The parade's passed us by." She shook her head sadly. "Funny. Nobody knew we used to sneak out of the house late at night and take long walks, hidden behind cloaks and veils." A small smile appeared. "Then that day Ramona took sick and I went to the drugstore, and there was the Pied Piper having an ice cream soda . . . and he talked to me . . . and then he brought Sylvia around . . . and then even got through to Ramona. And then Madame Vilna . . ." She stopped abruptly. "Please go. I better see to Ramona."

She led Max and Lockwood to the front door, and opened it. "Max." Their eyes met. "I'm sorry. It was none of my business."

Max mustered a smile and what he hoped was a friendly wink, and followed the silent Lockwood out. Chloe stood in the doorway and watched the retreating figures until they passed through the gate. She shut the door, bolted it and walked slowly to the kitchen.

"Well, *Ramona,*" she said cheerfully to the pensive figure seated at the table, "all over with?"

"All over with." The voice was tired and hoarse.

Chloe came behind the chair and placed her hands on the trembling shoulders. "Your nerves are shot. Would you like a drink?"

"Yes."

"We could both use a drink." She crossed to the liquor cabinet, knelt, opened it and found a bottle of Scotch.

"It's going to be very touch-and-go for the next few days," said Chloe as she poured the drinks. "Lockwood's no fool."

"Nor am I, darling, nor am I."

Gypsy Marie looked up from her Dream Book as the door to the store opened and a little man in a Chesterfield coat and a black derby entered brandishing a cane.

"Hiya, Gyp!" His voice needed oiling.

"Shut the door," she said solemnly.

"Seen Piper around?" he asked, moving to a chair.

"No. Let me see your palm."

He held out his right hand automatically as with his left he reached into a coat pocket and extracted a bag of candy. "I've got fifty for him."

Gypsy Marie looked at the little man narrowly. "Piper bets the ponies?"

"Oh sure," said the little man, popping a lemon ball into his mouth. "A twosie here, a fivesie there. Finally hit one today. Fiver on a ten-to-one shot and it came in. Solon's Girl in the fifth." He crunched down on the candy and savored the juices. "Had a hunch that finally paid off."

So, thought Gypsy Marie as she resumed studying the little man's palm, our Pied Piper has a vice after all. Horses yet. She shrugged. Why not? Man does not live by bread alone.

The little man addressed the top of her head. "This one on the house?"

She nodded slowly. "Beware a serious illness."

"Where's that?"

She pointed to a short line.

The little man peered at it. "That's a scratch, you nut."

Gypsy Marie shoved his hand away.

The little man laughed. "When are you gonna move you and your kid out of this hole?"

"When someone like you backs me in a tearoom. What do you say, Simon?"

"Simon says no. Sorry, kid. Smart bookies take bets. They don't make 'em. Have a candy."

"Back me, Simon. I'll pay off."

"Why don't you put the touch on those nutty Grace Sisters? They like you. They like the kid. Toss it around for a while. It might come up heads."

The Grace Sisters. It had never occurred to her. "You know," she said with a sudden feeling of elation, "that never occurred to me. I just wonder."

"Never wonder. Act." He spoke briskly and with self-assurance. "Look at me. Fifteen years ago I was getting nowhere in the garment trade. Then I go to Florida, get drunk with a gambling man, he takes a shine to me, teaches me the ropes, I abandon Audrey and the kids, and today I'm a happy and prosperous man two steps ahead of the cops." He lurched forward with his fists clenched. "Grab opportunity by the throat, that's Simon Winkle's motto. By the *throat!*" He pushed the bag of candy toward her. "That's for the kid. Tell him to shake the bag. The gumdrops are on the bottom." He was on his feet and at the door in three brisk movements.

"If you run into Quasi, send him home. He hasn't had his dinner."

"Rightee-oh, doll . . . and if Piper drops by, tell him I'm looking for him. I'll be hoisting a few at Whyte's." He was out as swiftly as he had entered.

The Grace Sisters.

Gypsy Marie drew the crystal ball closer and peered into it. "Once," she murmured, "just once . . . show me some *hope*."

"Stop *fussing* and sit *down!*" boomed Madame Vilna. She had endured ten minutes of silence, comfortably ensconced in the large, overstuffed easy chair that Max Van Larsen favored, watching Sylvia Plotkin bustling about the room like a small tornado in search of a village to raze. Sylvia had plumped and replumped pillows, emptied ashtrays and rearranged chairs, pausing every so often to pop a cold canapé in her mouth more out of nervousness than hunger. "It is at least an hour before the others will arrive."

Sylvia hurled herself onto the couch face down, with one eye and half a mouth visible. "I'm through with Max."

"*Mazel tov.*"

"I *really* mean it." She sat up, reached for another canapé and let her hand freeze in mid-reach as she caught the older woman's admonishing look.

"Leave some for your guests." The suggestion emerged like a drum roll. "I am feeling very ominous."

"What ominous?" Sylvia asked, lighting a cigarette.

"Danger ominous. I feel I am sitting in the path of a threat."

"Oh, stop it, Madame Vilna. Just because you caught the boy looking in your window . . ."

"He is unimportant."

(How true. How sad.)

"What I feel"—she clutched her ample bosom dramatically—"emanates from Ramona Grace."

Sylvia's right hand gave battle to a cloud of smoke attacking her eyes.

"What lies behind her mask?"

"Ugly scars," said Sylvia, eyes smarting.

"The *real* mask." Madame Vilna was rummaging in her purse, a second cousin to a carpetbag, and found a cigarette holder and a box of Turkish cigarettes. "Today . . ." she said darkly, "today I looked piercingly into her cold gray eyes, and for a fleeting moment"—she struck a kitchen match under the arm of the chair while Sylvia squelched a yelp—"I peered into the black inner recess of her soul. When you asked me to involve her in my readings, my instincts told me to refuse. But"—she paused to light the cigarette—"I *adore* you, Sylvia Plotkin, and I acquiesced. I have since spent many hours with her . . . and she is not *real*." She punctuated the sentence by leaning forward and fixing Sylvia hypnotically.

"What do you *mean* not real?" asked Sylvia innocently. "She's Ramona Grace! A sad, disfigured old recluse who's just emerged from her shell. Give her time to acclimate!"

Madame Vilna shook her head from side to side slowly. "She is frightened. She has a past."

"Well, of course she does! Everybody knows they were show girls and consorted"—a word she hated—"with gangsters. But that's water under the bridge. Now they're just two sweet old ladies. The Pied Piper calls them innocent doves. Isn't that sweet?"

"He is not real either," said Madame Vilna flatly.

"Professional jealousy."

"*Pfah!*"

"Don't *pfah* me." There was a wicked look on Sylvia's face. "You asked him to do some readings with you and he wouldn't. He told me. You didn't like that."

"He is obsequious."

"Nonsense. He's just grateful for small favors. All those years, a ship without a port. Now he's found a happy little harbor . . ."

"You sound like Arlene Francis," said Madame Vilna with a snort. "Ship without a port . . . happy little harbor . . . such poverty-stricken phrases." She leaped to her feet in one agile movement. "He's a bum who found a steady hand-out!"

"Oh, stop!" Sylvia's anger was genuine. "The poor old thing took the job I got him, didn't he? He makes a living . . ." as an afterthought, adding, "barely. What do you expect a man of that age to do anyway? What's gotten *into* you? I've never seen you like this before. You don't like Ramona . . . you don't like the Pied Piper . . ."

"I said *that?*"

Sylvia exhaled wearily.

"I did not say I *disliked* them. I said they are not *real!*"

She pleaded with the Modigliani print hanging over Sylvia's head. "Why does she misunderstand me? To say a person is not real is to express dislike? I *adore* Ramona. I *treasure* the Pied Piper." She stared at Sylvia. "But they are not real." She marched back to the easy chair, and like a ferryboat maneuvering into a slip, made herself comfortable. "I can assure you, my dear Sylvia Plotkin, my instincts are far more infallible than your Gypsy Marie's crystal ball. Ramona refuses to remove the mask for the reading. I have decided to let that pass. But have you noticed something that she and the Pied Piper have in common? They cannot walk down a street without constantly peering over their shoulders." She paused to let the comment sink in.

Sylvia was at a complete loss. "What has all this got to do with you?"

"*That,*" shouted Madame Vilna, "is what is driving me *mad!*" She puffed furiously at the Turkish cigarette, and Sylvia wondered if opening a window would offend her. "I feel," continued Madame Vilna, "that inadvertently both have said things in my presence they have later regretted saying! When I asked the Pied Piper to read with me, I suggested Poe . . . Edgar Allan of course. 'The Tell-Tale Heart.' And what he said at the time I recall disturbed me."

"What did he say?"

Madame Vilna slapped her thigh viciously. "That's what I can't remember! But today, just prior to my pleading with Ramona to remove her mask for the reading, I suggested we do a scene from *Gehargeteh Alter Menschen,* which perhaps you recall as *Arsenic and Old Lace,* and she reacted, to say the least, strangely. She said"—Madame Vilna drew herself up, hand over her mouth to simulate Ramona's surgical mask, eyes piercing—and for a moment Sylvia could have sworn it was Ramona Grace herself—"she said, 'I've had enough of dead bodies.' "

"So?"

Madame Vilna sighed with defeat. "Forget it." She sank back into the chair. "Perhaps I overreact. It is a sign of age. I am an old woman. A very tired, very worn old woman."

Sylvia crossed to her, knelt at her side with her arms around her. "You're younger than all of us."

Madame Vilna brightened considerably as she responded to Sylvia's embrace. "You are of course quite right, my dear Sylvia. Quite right."

But somewhere, dear Sylvia, there is a threat. I know it. I feel it. And when the opportunity arises, I shall tell Van Larsen. His soul broods like mine and he will understand.

C H A P T E R **VI**

*"Yo-ho-tay-hooooooo . . .
Yo-ho-tay-hooooooo . . .
Yo-ho . . . Yo-hooooooo . . ."*

The war cry of the Valkyries sadistically tortured the air of the soundproof room. The soundproofing had occurred some thirty years past when Lita Swenson Kramer's Brooklyn neighbors had petitioned the local authorities to have their city block declared a disaster area. Now, anywhere from three to eight hours daily, Lita Swenson Kramer reveled in her private recitals. She was her own star and her own audience, and neither was ever dissatisfied. Over the decades her repertoire expanded from Carmen to Mimi to Delilah to Lucia di Lammermoor. Then a brief skirmish with Butterfly, a bloodless battle with Tosca, a brutal raid on Manon, and at last, at the age of sixty-two, the death-defying challenge of Brunhilde. Somewhere waiting in the wings and cowering was La Sonnambula. Anything Sutherland could do she could do better, and she frequently told this to the looking glass which faced her atop the grand piano. The looking glass was guaranteed shatterproof.

It reflected a thin-lipped mouth, a whisper of a nose, which in profile disappeared completely (Lita frequently recalled the morning following her third session with plastic surgery, when she sharply admonished her doctor, "Milton . . . you've gone too far!"), two hazelnuts she accepted as eyes, carefully bordered with blue-green mascara, two pencil slashes that passed for eyebrows, and a blond bird's nest that had caused her hairdresser to be hospitalized with angina on twelve occasions.

Lita was a completely happy woman.

She paused in her recital to wipe the framed photo of her idol, Florence Foster Jenkins, and then resumed her attack on the piano and Wagner. As she sang, she phrased and rephrased in her mind the letter she'd been composing most of the afternoon. Surely Rudolph Bing couldn't continue to deny her a private audition. She had been in nightly attendance the previous season at the Metropolitan, and Bing *definitely* was in trouble. There had been no Callas, and even if there had been, what little voice was left would have shown signs of disintegration due to all that sea air from traveling on that yacht with that Greek. And surely no one could continue to take Leontyne Price seriously. She just *might* survive another season, and then after that, Las Vegas. Peters was aging rapidly, Resnick would never fulfill her earlier promise, and like a true Valkyrie, Lita Swenson Kramer to the rescue.

> *"Yo-ho-tay-hoooooo . . .*
> *Yo-ho-tay-hoooooo . . .*
> *Yo-ho . . . Yo-hoooooooooo . . ."*

She stopped abruptly. Her wristwatch said eight-fifteen. He must be upstairs and waiting. He's always prompt. Poor dear crippled darling. She stared at her reflection contentedly (true beauty never fades, it only enriches with the years, and you, Lita Swenson Kramer, are immortal), carefully rearranged three straws in the bird's nest, carefully lowered the lid over the piano keys (keys yellow with age, but never Lita Swenson Kramer), rose and crossed to the door with dainty fairy steps, opened the door and entered the basement playroom. Ten more fairy steps and she was in her private elevator. She pressed the button "M" and in thirty seconds emerged into the forty-foot living room.

The old man sat in an easy chair under a portrait of Schumann-Heink, warming a snifter of brandy with both arthritic hands. On the floor at his feet lay two iron hand crutches. He was eighty-one years old but could have passed for sixty. The topography of his face featured an aquiline nose, piercing green eyes, a broad and lavish mouth adorned by a neatly trimmed and waxed mustache. His huge mane of white hair was appended on each cheek with white mutton chops. He lowered the snifter when Lily appeared.

"What kept you?" he thundered.

"Wagner," she pizzicatoed.

"Come sit at my feet."

"Always, my precious."

With the grace of a teen-aged girl she pirouetted across the room and settled at his feet. He cupped her chin with his hand and whispered softly, "I miss your nose."

"I miss my career," she said with impassioned fervor. "I want to come back. I'm at my prime. God gave this gift and meant me to share it with the world. I *belong* to the world."

"You belong to me," he stated flatly, "and I'm not going to have you chased around your dressing room by a bunch of horny wop tenors." Lita pouted. He sipped the brandy, rolled it around in his mouth and swallowed. "Now tell me about the phone call."

Lita drew her knees up and clasped her hands around them. "It was about an hour ago. A man named Burton Lockwood. A parole officer from San Francisco."

There was a pleased expression on his face. "They're closing in on Roscoe. They'll find him for me, and when they do . . ." He ran an index finger menacingly across his throat. "He's double-exed me once too often."

"Now why should this Lockwood person think I could lead him to Roscoe?"

"That's how cops operate, my nightingale. Lots of dead ends until they come to a through street. I should have known better than to trust Roscoe this time. But still, after his stretch in stir, I'd figured he'd learned his lesson." He slammed his free hand down on the arm of the chair. "I've *got* to find Nola Kemp."

Lita screamed, "Don't *mention* that name! I wish you'd never *told* me about her. Armand cheating on me. *Me!* A prima donna!" He found her even more delicious when she bristled. She was shaking her head sadly. "How did he manage to outfox you. How? You . . . the brilliance of a Metternich . . . the genius of a Machiavelli . . . the shrewdness of a Rasputin."

"I was a shmuck." He placed the snifter on an end table and stroked his chin thoughtfully. "I often wonder if he's still alive."

"Armand? I hardly think so." She turned over and lay stomach-flat on a white bearskin rug, her chin resting on the bear's head. "He would have dropped me a postcard."

"Silly goose."

Lita giggled. She recalled her shy, quiet, withdrawn husband, carefully buying up parcels of land from the city dirt-cheap, carefully placing them in Nola Kemp's name. She sat up. "I didn't know what I had when I had it, did I, my Rudolfo."

"We were all too smug. How carefully I made it look I was Armand's front. And how beautifully he used it. July twenty-eighth, nineteen hundred and thirty two. How he must have waited for that day. The big haul. The big transaction. The purchase of that property in Nola's name. And before he transfers it to me, he disappears. And Nola Kemp knows where he is. Mark my words. She knows. He gave her that church."

"She sold it to Ramona."

"I remember the day Ramona came to my office with the transfer and Nola's signature. That surgical mask covering her face. Insisting I work a deal to keep Nola's name on the title. I wonder. I just wonder."

"What?"

"Would Ramona know Nola's whereabouts. Nola must have needed money badly to sell as cheaply as she did. Ramona gave me some cock-and-bull that Nola was heading for France. But I don't know. I just don't know. Ramona never lacked for brains either. Still . . . she and that dizzy sister of hers holed themselves up for the rest of their lives. But if Roscoe comes to anyone, he'll come to Chloe. His beloved Chloe."

"How do I handle Lockwood?"

"When?"

"Tomorrow morning. Oh dear." She rearranged herself on the floor with her legs crossed, looking like the world's oldest campfire girl. "He's coming to see me with another man. Van something."

"Larsen. Max Van Larsen."

"Oh pooh. Who told you?"

"Simon Winkle. I trained him well. He's kept his little network of spies very busy. Van Larsen and Lockwood visited the Grace girls a couple of hours ago. You've nothing to worry about. You're dead end."

"Not altogether." She cocked her head coquettishly. "Mr. Lockwood mentioned the name Morgan Montescue."

"What does he want with Morgan Montescue?"

"He thinks Roscoe Mears might be looking for him."

"Really!" He roared with laughter. "What fools! What complete and utter fools! *I'm* the *last* person Roscoe wants to see! He wants Nola and that . . . that *cash* Armand supposedly disappeared with. How could anyone disappear so completely?" he said with a heavy sigh.

"You've done it," she said with a twinkle in her voice. "You've been right under their noses all the time."

"That's the easiest place to hide, my lark. Right under their noses. Oh God," he said with a groan, "one last coup. That's all I ask for before I die. To find those deeds and make that sale back to the city. Ten million dollars. That's what they're worth. Ten million dollars."

"Would Ramona sell the church?"

"If necessary, I could persuade her. But if the Historical Society gets the ruin declared a landmark, they'd have to build around it. The church is the least of my worries. It's the city block surrounding it. Armand Kramer's city block in Nola's name."

"Roscoe doesn't know any of this, does he?"

"Nothing. He only knows about some missing cash he wants to lay his hands on. He wants to get out of the country. I had him sprung because he insisted that if Nola's alive, he could find her. I still think he can find her. The trick now is finding *him*. So tomorrow, with Lockwood and Van Larsen, play along."

"I shall play magnificently."

"And no recital."

"Not even *Un Bel Di Vendremo?*"

"No. But I have an idea how to lure Roscoe into the open. That's how we use Lockwood and Van Larsen. More brandy, please."

Okay okay okay!

You think you got me trapped back here, but you ain't! I'm too fast for you! Go ahead—try circling me from behind. I'll jump for that branch and swing myself up and then like a tightrope I'll walk the branch to the wall and jump over it and then I'll find Max and tell him what I saw!

I saw what you did! Bad! Bad! Naughty!

Here comes one. Come on. Come on. I'm ready for you!

Oh ho! I see what the other one's doing. Picking up that piece of wood. Sock me from behind. Like fun. Okay okay okay. Ready: Allez-oop!

"Grab his legs! Grab his legs!"

Ha! Made it! Now I'll walk the branch to the wall.

"Ha! Ha! You can't catch me! Ha! Ha! You can't catch me! I saw what you did! I'm telling the cops! Ha haaaaa . . ."

With a sickening crunch, the dried branch cracked, sagged, and then under the little hunchback's weight, crashed to the ground. The stick of wood struck him a glancing blow as he lay on the ground.

"Is he dead?"

"No. Take his legs. I'll grab him under the shoulders."

"What do we do with him?"

"We lock him up. And we keep him locked up . . . until we're ready. Don't stand there staring at me! Grab his legs!"

"Do you come here often?"

Edna St. Thomas Shelley groaned inwardly. She knew from the moment the dapper little man with the Chesterfield coat, cane and black derby sat on the stool next to her he would attempt to strike up a conversation. What, she wondered, is my particular allure to small men? Why don't truck drivers or stevedores find me tasty? Why this little man and not the one sitting on my right? I've brushed his knee six times with mine and no amount of "Excuse me's" or "Oh, I'm so sorry's" gets any response but a Neanderthal grunt. So what if his skin is mottled and his eyebrows need combing, he's *big*. I like my men *big*— She dug the olive out of her martini and punished it with her teeth.

"Here!" said her dapper little assailant, "have mine."

She watched glumly as, uninvited, with tiny thumb and tiny index finger he dropped a tiny olive into her glass. She fixed him with a withering look. "That's unsanitary."

The little man grinned. "Just had 'em manicured. Do you come here often?"

"Not any longer."

"You've been scowling from the moment I sat down."

"I don't scowl. That's my face."

"You live around here?"

"You're invading my privacy."

"Don't take offense. I'm absolutely harmless. You look like

an intelligent woman and I like to talk to intelligent women."

"Excuse me," said Edna to the obelisk on her right as she brushed his knee for the seventh time. She heard something that sounded like "urmph."

"What line of work you in?"

"Are you trying to pick me up?"

"Gee, you're a fast worker."

Beaten, Edna signaled for another martini.

"I'd like to buy that one."

"I buy my own," snapped Edna. "I do not come here often. I do not live around here. I'm an editor with a publishing company."

"Hey! I'm writing a book!"

Edna's shoulders sagged.

"Would you like to come up to my place and I'll read the first seven chapters to you?"

"I *loathe* being read to."

The bartender arrived with the fresh martini.

"Hey, Monkey." The little man was addressing the bartender. "The Pied Piper been around?"

Edna's ears perked up.

The bartender said, "No."

"If you see him, tell him I'm looking for him. He hit a winner today."

"Are you a bookie?" asked Edna.

The little man nodded proudly. "I do dabble in the dobbins."

"Got any hot tips?"

"Yeah. Come on up to my place."

"I appreciate the offer, but I'm due at a friend's house to watch her on television."

"Oh yeah? I guess a gal in your position always hobnobs with celebrities."

"Of a certain ilk, yes. This one happens to be Sylvia Plotkin."

"Ahhhhhhh!" said the little man as though he were appraising the Hope diamond. "Now *there's* a doll for you."

"Yes. Sylvia's a dear."

"Great book she wrote. Just great. How's the musical coming along?"

Edna paled. *"What* musical?"

"The one she's working on with Chloe Grace."

"I didn't know they were working on one." Chloe Grace!

"Oh sure. Old Chloe's got a trunk full of unpublished songs. What do you think she kept herself busy with all them years behind them walls?"

"Needlepoint."

"It was the Pied Piper's idea."

"Was it really? You seem to know everything that's going on around here."

He nudged her with his elbow as he winked conspiratorially. "It's my business to keep my eyes open."

And your mouth, Edna was tempted to add. "I'll bet you know a lot about the Grace Sisters."

"Some," he said modestly.

"Well, just this afternoon I told Sylvia I think there's a book in them."

"Wow, is there!"

"Wow really?"

"Take an awful lot of digging. They still keep pretty close-mouthed."

"They've gotten very friendly with Sylvia."

"There's friendly and there's friendly, right?"

"Right. My father used to say that all the time. They were his dying words. They're friendly with the Pied Piper too, aren't they?"

"Chloe is."

"And not Ramona?"

"Ramona's a tough old bird. She don't trust anybody. Spooky old broad, with that wild blue hair and that crazy surgical mask. They say some mobster cut her up a long time ago. Of course, that's very apocryphal." He grinned. "I had two years of college."

"I wonder," Edna mused aloud, "if they'd cooperate on a

book about themselves."

"You can't get killed for trying." He sipped his drink as Edna submerged in thought. "The Pied Piper might break the ice for you. With Chloe anyway. Ever meet him?"

"Once. Just once. Strange old duck. I wonder if he's for real."

"Yeah, I find him food for thought every so often myself. Like—what's his real name? Where does he come from? Who pays the funeral costs when he goes?"

"Have you tried asking?"

"Often. But he don't give much. He seems to talk to Chloe a lot, but she don't give much either. Funny, them suddenly coming out of seclusion just like that." He snapped his fingers, and from her right Edna again heard "urmph."

"According to Chloe, it was the Pied Piper's doing."

"Yeah? No kidding? Interesting. Very interesting."

"I thought you knew everything."

He winked again. "I do now. Excuse me a minute, will yah? I gotta make a phone call."

Do you know how to dial? wondered Edna. Her eyes followed him as he elbowed his way through the crowded bar to the phone booths in the rear. And then she spotted Max Van Larsen and another man.

"Bartender," said Edna brusquely, "my check."

Ow ow ow. My head my head my head. It hurts it hurts it hurts. Okay okay okay.

Quasimodo stirred and his eyes fluttered open. He was lying on a cement floor and it was damp and cold. His head hurt and his hump ached and his body was chilled. Slowly he pushed himself up to a sitting position and stared at his cramped surroundings.

He was in a small room the size of a prison cell. There was a heavy wooden door at one end, and at the other, an oval window with bars over it. There was a straw mattress on the floor and a blanket and a slop pail and a pitcher of water and a tin cup. There was an old steamer trunk and some battered valises piled on top of it. The walls of the room were cracked and from one of the cracks came a little trickle of water.

Okay okay okay. So you think you're getting away with this. That's what you think. Mama'll look into her crystal ball and find me. She'll see me there and come for me and wow . . . will your get yours. Okay okay okay.

Where am I?

He scrambled to his feet and peered up at the window. He rubbed his head and cursed an old gypsy oath under his breath. He moved to the valises, piled them on the floor, then dragged the steamer trunk to the window. He scrambled atop the trunk and looked out.

Okay okay okay.

I know where I am. What a view! I know where I am. Now I'll concentrate on Mama. I'll think of her. I'll think hard. Real hard. Then she'll feel I'm in trouble. She'll come to me. She'll save me. And then I'll join a circus.

He sat down on the trunk with his legs folded under him, his fists tightly clenched and his eyes shut.

Mama. Mama. It's me. It's Quasi. I'm in trouble. I'm still alive, but maybe not for long.

Mama. Mama, come to me. Find me. I love you, Mama.

"They say this stuff could be poisonous."

Max handed the artificial sweetener to Lockwood. "They say just about everything is poisonous," commented the parole officer as he carefully measured two drops into his cup, "but there's nothing as fatal as people." He shifted in his seat and slowly stirred his coffee. "A penny for them."

Max surfaced from his brief reverie. "I was contemplating the feminine mystique. To wit, the Sisters Grace. What makes two beauties suddenly decide to cut themselves off from the world for the rest of their lives. Obviously, at the time they were devoted to each other. It would have to be a very strong bond to make two people enter into that kind of pact." He paused for a moment. "Ramona's disfigurement. It must have occurred sometime during the period of Kramer's disappearance. Their last *Follies* appearance was in the nineteen thirty-one edition."

"It ran from the fall of thirty-one through the early spring of thirty-two," Lockwood said.

Max sipped his coffee. It was lukewarm and too sweet. He

married the cup to the saucer, pushed both to one side and lit a cigarette. "The show closes and that's the last of Nola Kemp. Shortly afterward we lose Judge Kramer. Then the Graces acquire the church from Nola either directly or through an intermediary . . ."

"Possibly Morgan Montescue."

". . . Possibly. And then Roscoe Mears is sent to San Francisco and tops the trip with a stretch in San Quentin. Lily Swenson Kramer enters a sanitarium. And finally Morgan Montescue chooses to lose himself in a sudden and very effective anonymity. An attempt is made on Roscoe's life in jail. Now we skip a few decades. Montescue gets Roscoe sprung, and then Roscoe evaporates. Finally, six months ago, due presumably to the blandishments of a very sweet old storyteller, the Sisters Grace decide to open the shutters, let the sun in and suffer the brave new world along with the rest of us pigeons."

"A man of special talents, your Pied Piper."

Max smiled. "I think the guy's blessed, in a funny way. He weaves a special brand of innocent magic, and I'm not that easily enchanted. He works wonders with kids."

"He works wonders with the Grace Sisters. I'd like to ask him for his recipe." Lockwood was applying a match to a cigar. "Max, you don't know a thing about the guy's background, do you?"

"Nothing."

"Then anything stands to reason, doesn't it? I mean this is simply conjecture. You know how it is in our line of work. You have a methodical mind. Me, I write little notes to myself on pieces of paper and then five days later wonder what the hell I had in mind. Now here's a little note I'm dropping. The Pied Piper tootles his flute and the kids come running. It's a special melody that even affects the tone-deaf. He adds an arpeggio and out fly the Sisters Grace. You say you know nothing about the Pied Piper's past. Any reason why he couldn't have been around New York some thirty-six years ago?"

"Anything's possible," Max said.

Lockwood studied the lighted end of the cigar. "It's just a thought, mind you. You see, Max, like I told you earlier today, there's more to Roscoe Mears then just parole-jumping. Ordinarily, you sit around and wait for the guy to make a false move, which sooner or later they usually do, and then get him delivered back parcel post. But it's been a year since I lost Roscoe, and in the interim, no false move. We know sooner or later he has to end up in New York, rainbow's end, the pot of gold. That means he's worked out a plan. A way of getting in and out undetected. But we know the one about the best-laid plans et cetera."

Lockwood leaned on the table with his arms folded. "Roscoe might have hit a snag. Missed a connection here or there. Something's holding him up. If he's gotten into trouble under an assumed name, we'd have known about it. His fingerprints would have been checked out with Washington. So we can scratch that." He tapped the table firmly with an index finger. "He's right here in New York. I think he's been here for quite a while. By rights, he should have made contact with Chloe Grace by now, yet she says he hasn't."

"She sounded like she preferred he didn't," Max said.

"That's how she sounded, but don't trust all the sounds you hear. Those ladies are on edge. A tea tray crashes. They snipe at each other. One goes into a snit in the kitchen and starts busting up the place. Our ladies are on edge, Max. The name Roscoe Mears unnerves them. After almost four decades, why? They sound like this is the first they know Roscoe is on the loose. When he was sprung fifteen months ago, it never made the papers. Montescue's shyster saw to that. Now I appear on their doorstep with you. I mention names they don't want to hear mentioned. Roscoe. Nola. Montescue. Lita Kramer. The judge. A lot of untasty old chickens coming home to roost. Something's got to give. A seam's got to burst and out of that seam has to pop friend Roscoe."

Max wondered why his sudden feeling of elation. Why was his pulse pounding and his fingertips tingling? It was the delicious old excitement. That Fourth of July feeling of firecrackers exploding and a shower of sparklers, the hunter's instinct that he might bag more then his share of game. "Burton," said Max, almost singing the name, "do you suppose it's sometimes possible to solve the mystery of a thirty-six-year-old disappearance?"

"Max," said Burton, "the minute I first shook your hand, I knew we were meant for each other. As the old maid said to the rapist, this is more than I expected. Now Roscoe's a fairly clever devil." He inundated the area with four swift puffs of cigar smoke, and a lady at an adjoining table waved her handkerchief like a stormswept semaphor. "Supposing I'm Roscoe. I make it safely across the country to New York. I have to hole up. Bide my time. I have an idea how to lay my hands on a hidden fortune, but I have to be patient, cautious, move slowly and patiently. I have to beware of two adversaries, the police and Morgan Montescue. Why Montescue's so hot for Roscoe we don't know. Maybe Lily Kramer will inadvertently help with that. But we're safe in surmising it's got something to do with our missing judge—I, Roscoe, know a few things. To somebody that's dangerous, to somebody else that's useful. I was attacked in stir and almost murdered. Those wouldn't have been Montescue's orders. He obviously wants me alive. Why? Because I know how to find Nola Kemp. Why does Montescue want Nola unearthed?" Lockwood sighed. "We need Montescue for that one."

"Keep going," urged Max, "you're doing beautifully."

"I know. I could just hug myself with joy. Now here am I, Roscoe Mears, waiting for the right moment to contact a friend. Chloe Grace. Chloe says she was Rightie's girl. That might have something to do with Roscoe ending up in San Quentin. Now I wonder . . . whose girl was Ramona?" His eyes lit up. "Maybe we're barking up the wrong Grace!"

"But it was Ramona who said Roscoe was sweet on Chloe."

"Chloe denied it, didn't she? Damn it. I want to talk to Ramona Grace alone. Away from that house. Can you try and fix it?"

"Can do. There's a lovely old broad I'm chummy with named Madame Vilna. She used to be a big star in the Yiddish theater. She makes a living now giving dramatic readings. She always works with someone. At the moment, thanks again to the Pied Piper and a certain"—the muscles of his jaw tensed—"friend of mine, it's Ramona. I'll work it out with Madame Vilna."

"Good. The sooner the better. Something tells me all hell's going to break loose soon. Roscoe will soon know or already knows I'm in town. Funny. Very funny."

"What is?"

"Roscoe. When a guy gets out of stir, he usually reverts to his old habits and habitats. Saloons. Betting parlors. Old hangouts, if they still exist. Roscoe was a garrulous cuss. He liked an audience. He was a gambling man. He was a drinker. Could he really have disciplined himself so thoroughly into losing the old Roscoe? Maybe he could. All those years in jail gave him time to think and plot and devise. You know something, I'm beginning to admire the bastard!"

"Where'd the dame go?" Simon Winkle asked the bartender when he returned from the phone booth.

"She sashayed thataway."

The bookmaker turned and saw Edna St. Thomas Shelley zeroing in on a table at the far side of the room. He recognized Max Van Larsen and Burton Lockwood. Very carefully, with the air of a Beau Brummell, he placed his black derby on his head at a rakish angle, buttoned the Chesterfield coat, took a firm grip on his cane—and left.

Marianne Kahane was a short, dumpy, middle-aged woman whose motto was "Preservation!" An amateur ornithologist, she presided over a bird-preservation society. (Mondays) She fought to save the quail and the pheasant and other feathered delicacies from an extinction she was positive would soon equal the fate of the American buffalo. (Her Society to Preserve the American Buffalo met on Tuesdays.) Through the auspices of Sylvia Plotkin, Edna St. Thomas Shelley had read Miss Kahane's manuscript "Sex and the Single Gull" and then threatened Sylvia with a knife. On Wednesdays, Marianne Kahane worked to preserve the American Indian and had even been made an honorary squaw by the Shinnecock tribe out in Southampton, an honor she had gratefully repaid by purchasing some thirty dollars' worth of trinkets, most of which she later found stamped "Made in Japan." On Thursdays, her good efforts were confined to her home. She preserved fruits in cans and jars and stacked them on shelves in her cellar. She never ate them. She just preserved them.

Her most important preservational activities, however, were confined to what she considered to be historical landmarks. The reconverted church in which the Grace Sisters resided was her current baby, and she meant to nurse, diaper and feed it until it outsurvived even herself. Now it seemed victory was at hand, and she needed the cooperation of the Grace Sisters.

As she turned the corner into Catherine Slip, she saw Chloe emerging through the gateway.

"Miss Grace! Miss *Grace!*" Miss Kahane's voice had the piercing texture of a bosun's whistle piping the admiral aboard ship. It took wing with the rapidity of an anxious starling, and Chloe winced in dismay. Her hand tightened on the gate and she hastily slammed it shut. In the minute it took Miss Kahane to reach her side, Chloe had time to recompose her face, and it now reflected a passable expression of pleasure as the other woman reached her with puffed cheeks and intermittent wheezes.

"Victory! Victory is at hand!" wheezed Miss Kahane, and Chloe briefly entertained a vision of a Russian general pelting snowballs at a retreating Napoleon.

"Catch your breath, dear," intoned Chloe as she took the woman's arm and slowly walked her away from the gate

"It's been arranged for Saturday," puffed Miss Kahane. "And then victory will be ours!" She had deftly disengageu Chloe's hand and now had both talons firmly clamped on Chloe's shoulders. Chloe shuddered inwardly like a F: ach war hero about to be kissed on both cheeks by a garlic-breathed general.

"What's been arranged for Saturday?"

"The City Committee!" Chloe wondered if Ophelia had felt the way she did prior to taking the fatal dip. "The committee who pass on historical landmarks. They will tour your home on Saturday!"

"Oh," said Chloe slowly, drawing it out like a fresh piece of taffy, "that barely gives us time to tidy up."

"Tidy up? Tidy up?" (To arms! To arms!) "Why tidy up? What's to tidy up? In dissarray lies its charm! Now then", she continued cozily, "I've taken the liberty of laying out the tour." She rummaged in her mammoth purse, and Chloe heard two jars of preserves strike against each other. "Here it is." She waved a typewritten list and then fumbled in her purse until she extracted her bifocals. "Over here. The light's better." She pulled Chloe to a lamppost.

Stoically, Chloe listened to the details of the proposed tour. Cellar and subcellar, where runaway slaves were hidden over a century ago. Then vestry and chancel and apse and rectorate (emerging from Miss Kahane's mouth like Donder, Blitzen, Dancer and Prancer). Then bell tower and tower cells, and Chloe fought an urge to faint at her feet. Miss Kahane jammed list and bifocals back into her purse and beamed from ear to ear. "By Saturday noon you'll be safe from the wreckers!"

Chloe look startled. "What wreckers?"

"My dear, my dear." She had the benign expression of one of Agatha Christie's precious "pussies." "Don't you read the real estate sections of the newspaper? There's a plan afoot to convert this entire block into a municipal industrial building!

But if we succeed in convincing the City Committee to declare *you* a landmark, they will build *around* you! Don't you ever *read* real estate?"

"No." Chloe didn't recognize her own voice. "But my sister does."

"Your sister!" cried Miss Kahane as she clutched Chloe's arm. "We must go tell your sister! Why, Miss Grace. You're trembling. You're overcome. It's all too much for you."

"You have no idea. My sister's resting at the moment, Miss Kahane. I'll relay the good news later."

"Of course, of course." Miss Kahane patted Chloe's hand with gentle understanding. "But we must meet tomorrow to formulate Saturday. Will you phone me in the morning?"

"Yes."

"Oh!" She was back in the purse again. "And these are for you." She thrust the two jars at Chloe. "Kumquats."

"Just what I wanted."

"Call me in the morning! Don't forget! It'll be an easy night's sleep for you tonight, won't it!"

Chloe said nothing, and Miss Kahane accepted her silence as an emotional one. She flapped her arms and took off into the night. Slowly, clutching a jar in each hand, Chloe turned and walked to the gate. She leaned against it for a moment, deep in thought, and then unlatched it. Stiffly, she walked up the path and entered the house.

Burton Lockwood was astonished at how fast Edna St. Thomas Shelley's lips could move without ever leaving her face. Surely they would soon drop to the tablecloth like dried persimmons or hang alop like shutters in a hurricane. But Edna's lips were as firmly secure as her single-mindedness on any topic under discussion, and the topic of the moment was that current literary giantess Sylvia Plotkin.

In the fifteen minutes that ensued after she had wedged herself in at the table between Max and Lockwood, she had winnowed Lockwood's name, rank, serial number and pedigree, ferreted from the two Nimrods as much as they could possibly reveal about the missing Roscoe Mears, and then plunged with a glib ferocity into theoretics on the Grace Sisters, the Pied Piper and the dapper little bookie "who made a pass that would have put Joe Namath to shame." Max had no trouble identifying Simon Winkle.

Lockwood wondered what Edna's knee was trying to tell him. "Urmph," he murmured at one point of contact, and Edna thought to herself grimly, I have been here before.

In her fifteen minutes of solitude at the bar prior to Simon Winkle's onslaught, Edna had thoroughly redigested and revised her thinking on the Sylvia–Max impasse. Sylvia needed Max, Max needed Sylvia (she was about to tell him), and Edna needed Sylvia's new book.

"Now, Max," began Edna with a vivacity she usually reserved for book conventions, "there's absolutely no reason why you shouldn't continue with your book. Since you say yours is completely factual and Sylvia's is fiction, they can do nothing but *complement* each other. And she's drawn a *delicious* portrait of *you*." Max paled. "You're so good about her chicken soup. I *loathe* chicken soup." Max brightened. "I wouldn't rinse my undies in it. *Now*"—she nailed the word to Max's ear— "Sylvia's book needs a preface, a foreword, an introduction of some sort. *You're* the man to write it." Max moved to remonstrate, but Edna was too quick for him. "Don't interrupt. *You* broke the Tippy Blaney case, and in less than ten hours, which is absolutely heroic. And I know Sylvia will be *ecstatic* at the thought of you and her between covers together."

Max blushed, and Lockwood applied some pressure of his own to Edna's knee. Taking the opportunity to inhale, Edna flashed Lockwood a provocative smile that said little but promised much. Lockwood envisioned a window display of *Parole Officer* at Brentano's.

"Which brings me to a project I've been mulling over all day.

The Grace Sisters." She told them about the session earlier in the day at Schrafft's and her suggestion to Sylvia that there was a book in the Grace Sisters. Lockwood and Max listened with interest. "Max, I'm convinced if that book's to be written, it has to be a collaboration between you and Sylvia."

Max looked on the verge of exploding, and Edna's hand shot up in a gesture that would have stopped traffic on Broadway and Forty-second Street—and brought forth an anxious waiter, whom she summarily dismissed.

"Sylvia needs you, Max, and *you* need Sylvia." Max began bristling and opened his mouth, but the voice heard continued to be Edna's. "I'm absolutely *fed up* with people reluctant to admit their needs." Lockwood "urmphed" and Edna relaxed her knee. "I'm supremely confident you two clever creatures will bring Roscoe Arbuckle . . ."

". . . Mears," corrected Lockwood.

". . . Whatever," said Edna with an irritated toss of her head, "to bay and I'm convinced the Grace Sisters will figure in it importantly. What a juicy climax I foresee! What a cast of characters!" She slammed a hand down on the table. "Positively the Literary Guild. See it, Max. See it with my eyes."

And your mouth, thought Max. He found mouths replacing knees as the ugliest part of a woman's physiognomy.

Edna was busy ticking off the fingers of her left hand. "The Grace Sisters. Roscoe Mears. Judge Kramer. Gangsters. Theft." She switched to her right hand. "That Morgan somebody or other. The Pied Piper. Lily you-know." And then she pointed her index finger. "Murder."

Max leaned back in the chair. "Roscoe Mears is really Lockwood's case," he said.

Edna's head swiveled slowly to Lockwood and her eyes held his hypnotically. "I'll see that they dedicate the book to you."

"You'll do better than that," said Lockwood.

"Urmph," said Edna.

"I just finished writing a book of my own."

"You haven't." Her voice fell to the table like crumpled halvah.

"It's called *Parole Officer*. Would you do me the honor of reading it?"

Edna rallied. "I'd be delighted. Send it to my office."

"I've got it right here," said Lockwood, placing his briefcase on the table. Edna stared at it like a detonation expert.

Max broke the silence. "Sylvia and I aren't speaking."

"Easily mended," said Edna confidently. "We're going to her place right now."

"Oh no, I'm not!"

"Don't be a spoilsport. She's having an intimate party to watch the television show. You just let *me* handle *everything*. Burton would love to come too, wouldn't you, Burton?" Burton said he'd be delighted. "You'll have the Grace Sisters and the Pied Piper under one roof and it'll be interesting to study them together. And, Max, your appearance will *make* the evening for Sylvia."

"I'm not going."

"Max . . ."

"I said no."

Edna lit a cigarette.

"Urmph," Lockwood said.

The Pied Piper stood in the doorway of the room he used as living quarters in the basement of Robert Wagner High School. There was a glow from the naked bulb in the center of the ceiling, and there shouldn't have been. He never forgot to flip the switch when he left the room. As he shut the door slowly behind him, his eyes canvassed the room. He could tell he had had a visitor. The carton boxes containing his meager possessions had been disturbed. The door to the medicine chest was slightly ajar and the bedding on his cot was mussed. His books had been moved and a small case that contained private papers had been unsuccessfully jimmied. His eyes moved to an envelope on the table Sylvia Plotkin had appropriated from the school's lunchroom.

He tore the envelope open and withdrew five ten-dollar bills and a note on which was written in a tiny, precise script: "Your horse came in. What does the name Morgan Montescue mean to you? I'm at home watching Plotkin on TV."

The Pied Piper pocketed the money and the note, crumpled the envelope and flung it across the room, where it landed on the cot, pulled a cane-back chair toward him and sat.

"Morgan Montescue," he whispered, and the name drifted upward and spiraled and settled over his head like the sword of Damocles.

CHAPTER VIII

Gypsy Marie Rachmaninoff hurried along the street to Sylvia Plotkin's apartment house, the cold wind stinging her hands and face, her eyes smarting from the wind. One hand tightly clasped the ends of her shawl together, the other gripped a sewing basket, and a feeling of uneasiness was probing around in her brain like busy fingers at a rummage sale. Where was her son? Perhaps waiting for her at Sylvia's. Twice tonight, while preparing to leave for Sylvia's, she could have sworn she had heard Quasi calling her. She had opened the back window and looked out and then gone to the front door and looked up and down the street, but not a sign of the boy.

Then she had hurried to the high school and the possibility of finding Quasi with the Pied Piper. She encountered Simon Winkle, who told her the Pied Piper was out. She continued on her way to Sylvia's. In the future she would have to use a firmer hand with the boy. He's getting too old to look in windows. Childish pranks could lead to adult misdemeanors, and she wanted no unnecessary truck with the police. It could prove difficult to secure a license for the tearoom. If the Grace Sisters wouldn't back her—perhaps Sylvia? Sylvia was kind and good and understanding and making money.

Her thoughts returned to the boy. Was his deformity her punishment? An evil omen, the tribe whispered among themselves, and she and the boy were banished. Superstitious nomads. Only the elderly and the middle-aged remained. The youngsters abandoned camp for a better life. Soon the tribes would gather in New York for their annual Gyp-In. How they would scoff at her and her sad little store. But I survive, she told herself proudly, and I'm raising my boy on my own without resorting to pilfering and whoring. And one day that boy will make me proud of him.

Where is he? He hasn't had his supper. He's out here somewhere, cold and hungry and probably ruining his eyesight. A rush of anger engulfed her. When I lay my hands on him I'll kill him.

"What's keeping everybody!" Sylvia cried mournfully to Madame Vilna, beginning to feel like a blood sister to Stella Dallas. "The *hors d'oeuvres* are going dry. The chopped chicken liver is getting brown at the edges. Look at how the salami is curling up!"

Madame Vilna examined the salami. "You should have kept it in the refrigerator till they got here."

Sylvia slumped onto the couch, clasped her hands and fought back tears. "I invited them for an hour ahead of time. When my publisher poured for me, everybody was there *early*."

"Vultures," snorted Madame Vilna as she helped herself to another shot of slivovitz.

"The program starts in fifteen minutes!"

"Please, Sylvia," pleaded Madame Vilna, "my nerves have still not composed themselves and I am imbibing far too much of this slivovitz'"—downing the shot in one gulp and smacking her lips—"which in my present state I find utterly irresistible."

She poured another large shot. "It must be sun spots," she said. "Everyone seems in a state of discombobulation. Especially Vilna. Vilna, who has charisma, suddenly feels as colorless as this slivovitz. From the moment I caught that misanthrope staring in my window . . ."

"He's not a misanthrope!" Sylvia interjected. "If people would love him, he'd love them back." (I love you, Max. Now love me back.)

"From that very moment," continued Madame Vilna with a disdainful wave of her hand, "have I felt disoriented. I had the same feeling the night I made my entrance in *Farblungeter Vieber,* which perhaps you might recall as *The Cradle Snatchers,* and the juvenile fell dead at my feet from an embolism, as a hasty autopsy later proved."

Sylvia groaned and the doorbell chimed. "It's somebody!" she yelled, jumping to her feet, dashing to a wall mirror, patting her coiffure, pinching her cheeks, wetting her lips and sprinting past Madame Vilna to the door. Vilna downed her drink and poured another.

Sylvia was glaring at Edna St. Thomas Shelley. "What *kept* you? Do you realize the program starts in . . ." (Be still my heart.) She saw Max and another man.

Edna's nose wiggled saucily as she jauntily expostulated, "Never underestimate the power of a woman. On my left you have Burton Lockwood of the San Francisco police department. Sylvia, you're paralyzed."

Sylvia's knees were on the verge of buckling and she gripped the doorknob for support. "So nice to meet you, Mr. Lockwood," she managed to say. "Please come in the program starts in just a few minutes there's lots to eat and drink this is Madame Vilna a dear friend Edna you've changed your dress I love you in fuchsia not that chair Mr. Lockwood this chair you'll find it far more comfortable it's a Ward Bennett and not cheap can I fix you some chopped liver it's my mother's recipe may she rest in peace I'm not hello Max."

Max put his arms around her and kissed her cheek and then whispered in her ear, "I'm sorry."

"Excuse me," cried Sylvia as she dashed for the bedroom, grabbed a tissue from the box on her dresser—and burst into tears.

"Max!" shouted Vilna. "You are here! It is ESP, Max! We are surrounded by doom!"

"Vilnaaaaa!" trilled Sylvia from the bedroom.

"I will not be Vilnaed!" shouted Vilna as she breezed past the astonished and delighted Lockwood and caught Max in a bear hug. "I am surrounded by unreality and with unreality I cannot cope!" She released Max and turned to Lockwood as Edna saw to drinks. "I am flesh and blood and heart and soul and I grasp life by both ears! But today! Today! I am swamped by a most unnerving *arteefeeshialiteee!* You have a magnificent head, Mr. Lockwood. Have you ever contemplated a career in the theater? I can see you in *Ubgehockter Hent,* which perhaps is more familiar to you as *Titus Andronicus.* Max, later we must talk."

Sylvia swept back into the room.

"You've changed your dress," said Edna.

"I didn't want to clash with your fuchsia," gurgled their hostess, a vision in a low-cut green lace creation with an orange belt crested with purple rhinestones.

"It's lovely," said Max, who knew better than not to comment.

Sylvia smiled. "Eat something. I wonder what could be keeping the others."

The doorbell chimed.

"Hark," said Edna. She sat next to Lockwood, who soon said "Urmph" as Sylvia opened the door and Gypsy Marie Rachmaninoff entered.

"What *kept* you?" asked Sylvia.

"Where's Quasi?" was the response. "I'll wring his neck."

"You may call upon me for assistance," intoned Madame Vilna.

"He hasn't had his dinner," said Gypsy Marie to Sylvia.

"He can nosh when he gets here," said Sylvia gaily, her face beaming as she introduced Gypsy Marie to Lockwood.

Max was tuning in the television set and small talk erupted. The doorbell chimed again and Sylvia admitted Chloe Grace.

"What *kept* you?" asked Sylvia.

Chloe was staring past her at Max and Lockwood. "Ramona took ill suddenly."

Madame Vilna cried, "Oy!"

Chloe continued. "She took a sedative and went to bed. She'll be fine in the morning."

"She must be!" cried Madame Vilna. "Tomorrow we rehearse!"

Lockwood was falling in love with her but said "Urmph."

Edna helped herself to a piece of salami. "The salami's hard," she announced.

Sylvia flashed her a look, and for the first time in years Edna cringed. Max had the screen in focus but kept the sound down as he rejoined the others. Lockwood experienced a sudden chill as he felt ten fingers probing his head.

"You've been sapped five times," intoned Gypsy Marie huskily.

"Six," corrected Lockwood.

"Perhaps. You have a thick skull. You are versatile." She felt his ears. "Little escapes you."

Which was Edna's cue to launch into a brief dissertation on Lockwood's search for Roscoe Mears, Sylvia interspersing with "Really!" and "Do tell!" and "How fascinating!" until the doorbell chimed again.

"That better be Quasi," said Gypsy Marie as her fingers stiffened and Lockwood yelled "Ouch!"

It was the building superintendent with a package. He refused an invitation to watch the television show with Sylvia's guests, explained that the package had arrived earlier in the day but this was his first opportunity to deliver it, and after accepting a slice of bread smeared with chopped liver, departed.

Sylvia tore open the package and yelped with glee. "Look, everybody," she cried rapturously, "the French edition of my book!"

"The show's starting," said Max glumly and he turned up the sound.

Oh God, thought Sylvia as Edna examined one of the French editions and then passed it around to the others, my outburst! He'll see me breaking into tears! You rotten television set! Tonight of all nights must your reception be so clear and beautifully defined?

"Max dear," said Sylvia with a trembling sweetness, "fiddle with the color dial. The set's too green."

Max fiddled.

"Where's Piper?" asked Gypsy Marie of no one in particular.

"Piper!" exclaimed Sylvia. "I forgot all about him." She ran to the door and opened it as though the mention of his name would bring his appearance. Madame Vilna poured her eighth slivovitz and then gracefully settled onto the floor at Max's feet. Sylvia returned to her seat and said with perplexity, "He's always on time. He was especially looking forward to seeing the program. Don't shush me, Edna. We're on last. I wonder if I should phone the school?"

"He's probably out spending his money," suggested Gypsy Marie.

Sylvia's head jerked to her left. *"What* money?"

"He won fifty on a horse today. Simon Winkle told me."

Edna shuddered at the mention of the little man's name.

"Ramona and I are planning a trip," Chloe said.

All eyes were on her as Max wondered if Lockwood was thinking what he was thinking.

"Not until after the reading," intoned Madame Vilna darkly.

"We're thinking of Mexico," said Chloe. "For Ramona's nerves." She flashed a conspiratorial smile at Max. "She had a slight accident this evening." Lockwood shifted in his seat. "That's really why she took the sedative and went to bed. She burned her fingers on the teakettle during one of her snits. It was terribly painful, but you know Ramona."

Who knows Ramona? Madame Vilna thought to herself.

"The poor darling!" cried Sylvia. "Did you call a doctor?"

"She'd have none of it," said Chloe. "I applied some salve and bandaged her hands and I'm sure it'll be all right in a few days."

"God," snapped Edna, "now she's *all* bandages."

Sylvia flashed her a look and Edna gulped her drink.

"Bandages," muttered Madame Vilna. "The Workmen's Circle will have nightmares." She shook her head, clucked her tongue and downed the slivovitz.

"How soon were you planning to leave?" Max asked Chloe.

"In a few days. Saturday, actually."

"Saturday!" shrieked Vilna as she nimbly rose to her feet. "On Saturday we *read!*"

"Oh dear," said Chloe in a wisp of a voice, "then we'll go Sunday. Ramona's in such a *state!*"

"She will be in a *worssssse* state if she does not *read!*"

"She'll read." Chloe was fingering the pearls around her neck, and somehow they felt as coarse as rope.

"Guttenyoo," said Madame Vilna as she refilled her glass.

"I wish Piper would get here," Sylvia whispered to Max, and he took her hand and patted it gently. Sylvia wondered what was that melody in the distance and then realized it was her heart singing.

"I just don't understand Piper," she said. "I just don't understand him. He was so anxious to see the show." Max put his arm around her and Sylvia blessed the man who invented loveseats.

"That's us!" cried Edna.

"My name is Sylvia Plotkin . . ."

"My *name* is Sylvia Plotkin . . ."

Dapper little Simon Winkle sat sprawled in his little easy chair with his little arms dangling limply over the sides. His little feet were limply splayed on the rug and his little eyes stared unseeing at the little television set six feet away. Around his neck was his little scarf tied in the back with a little but extremely secure knot. His little tongue protruded slightly from his little mouth, and were a doctor to examine him at the moment, he would pronounce little hope.

There was a burst of laughter from the television set, but of course Simon Winkle's little ears were unhearing. They couldn't hear the footsteps crossing to the door, the door closing. They didn't hear "Will the *real* Sylvia Plotkin please stand up."

"Turn off the set! That's the end!" cried Sylvia as her image on the screen was struggling to rise. She was rushing for the set when Edna yelled, "That's not the end!" And too late a chagrined Sylvia watched herself burst into tears.

"Darling Sylvia," cried Madame Vilna, unaware she was slurring her words. "You were overcome."

"The excitement was too much for me," said Sylvia weakly.

Lockwood was at the bar mixing himself a drink, and Edna was massaging her knee. She thought she could hear the water lapping. Max had his arm around Sylvia and told her, "You were delightful. I'm proud of you." Sylvia raised her head and Max kissed her cheek.

"How about that con on TV!" Lockwood expostulated. "From safecracker to wisecracker." He was referring to the program panelist who had known an earlier fame as a felon. "If Roscoe Mears had used his head, he could have gotten himself booked on *Hollywood Palace* instead of taking it on the lam."

Chloe began nodding as he spoke. "I agree with you. Roscoe might have cashed in. There would have been human interest in him and talent with which to back it up."

"Talk about talent," interrupted Edna, "what's this jazz, Sylvia, about you and Chloe doing a musical version of *May I Leave the Room?*"

"Why not?" asked Sylvia with a shrug of innocence.

"Well, hell, if you want to do a musical you get . . ."

". . . A more important composer," said Chloe with an understanding smile. "I have to bow out, anyway, Sylvia. There's no telling how long Ramona and I will be gone."

"What about your house?" asked Sylvia. "Who'll look after your interests?"

"Ramona is considering selling."

Max caught that, and his eyes met Lockwood's.

"Really planning to start out fresh, eh, Miss Grace?" said Lockwood.

"It's never too late for a new life. It took a lot of persuasion, but Ramona finally sees it my way. However, nothing's really definite. May I have another sherry, Sylvia?"

"Who would you sell to?" persisted Lockwood.

"The city," replied Chloe. "They're trying to buy up the entire block for an industrial complex."

"Miss Kahane will be shattered," said Sylvia. "She's fought so hard and so long to have the place declared a historical landmark."

"Miss Kahane likes a good battle," said Chloe with a smile. "If we sell, she can go fight City Hall."

Gypsy Marie stuck a finger with the needle and yelped. "Blood," she whispered eerily as a tiny bead appeared. "Blood." She stuck the finger in her mouth, then dropped everything into the sewing basket and snapped it shut. "I must go look for Quasimodo. I am a mother first and a gypsy second. A tiny voice inside me tells me he is in trouble." She looked to Max, and he recognized the appeal in her eyes. "Please, Max. Call the precinct and see if they've arrested any Peeping Toms."

"The precinct knows Quasimodo."

"Max," said Sylvia, "call." She crossed to Gypsy Marie and held her hand as Max dialed. "He's just upset, dear, that's all. He's probably off someplace brooding. Maybe Madame Vilna was a little too rough on him."

"*Rough!*" stormed Madame Vilna. "I was the soul of gentility! I should have boxed his ears and given him a good *potch* on the backside." Then she added with a lavish dramatic gesture, "But if any harm has befallen the poor misbegotten creature, a villain shall answer to me! Above all . . . I am a mother, and grandmother, and great-grandmother . . ." And her voice trailed away as Max hung up and turned to the room.

"Nothing," he stated simply.

"Then I must go look for him."

The doorbell chimed. Sylvia skipped to the door and opened it. "Piper! For shame! You're late! You missed the show!"

"Forgive me, Sylvia," he said as he entered, "but a pipe broke at the school. I was hours making repairs."

Gypsy Marie made a move to speak, but Max was in there ahead of her. "Quasimodo wasn't with you, by any chance?"

"Quasi? I haven't seen him all day. Ah, food! I'm famished."

Gypsy Marie intercepted his move. "You're sure? Quasi's upset. He always runs to you when he's upset."

"I've been in the school basement all evening. He would have found me."

"Simon Winkle didn't find you."

The Pied Piper began stroking his beard thoughtfully. "Was Simon Winkle looking for me?"

"I met him coming out of the school basement. I went there to look for my boy. Simon said you weren't there."

"Oh. That must have been when I went to the hardware store. I wasn't gone more than fifteen or twenty minutes. Now what would Simon Winkle want with me?"

"You foxy grandpa," said Max, "your horse came in."

The Pied Piper reddened. "Imagine. The first time in my life I gamble on a horse and it wins."

You foxy liar, thought Edna, but gracefully refrained from vocalizing it.

"Eat something," said Sylvia.

Gypsy Marie picked up the sewing basket and headed for the door. She opened it and then turned to Max. "Max, if you hear anything, you'll let me know right away, won't you?"

Edna restrained a chuckle. *Clouded crystal ball, Rachmaninoff?*

"Don't worry about him," said Max, "he's probably home waiting for you."

"He better be," said Gypsy Marie grimly, and left.

"Poor thing," said Sylvia, "she has her hands full with that boy."

Madame Vilna sighed and poured another slivovitz. Lockwood made his way to the Pied Piper, and Chloe stole a glance at her wristwatch. When she looked up, Max was smiling down at her.

"Sit down, Max," said Chloe, "I can't stand being hovered over.

Max sat. "This sudden decision to go to Mexico . . ." he said.

"What about it?"

"Level with me, Chloe. Are you and Ramona afraid of Roscoe Mears?"

Her eyes widened almost mockingly. "Whatever for? In the old days we were buddies. He even used us in his film, though we were only decorations. Oh, I see. Ramona's crack about Roscoe being sweet on me. Maybe he was. Lots of men had crushes on us. After all, with a little imagination, instead of two decrepit old bags you might envision a pair of long-stemmed beauties. And don't flatter me by saying I'm still good to look at. I'm not."

"Who disfigured Ramona?"

"That has nothing to do with finding Roscoe."

"What made you girls hole yourselves up all these years?"

"Why discuss it now?"

"Are you positive you can't give us a lead to Morgan Montescue?"

"Very positive."

The Pied Piper's laughter exploded over the room and he was

the center of attention. "Will you listen to the man," he said jocularly, pointing to Lockwood at his side. "He thinks in the nether world of the past even *I* might have known Roscoe Mears."

Chloe laughed.

"My good man," continued the Pied Piper, pounding Lockwood heartily on the shoulder, "as I recall that era, I was working my way through the southwest as an itinerant troubadour. I admit the present beard was then a mere stubble and my songs and stories a bit fresher. There, there! Don't look so chagrined. In your line of work, I understand no stone must be left unturned. Chloe! Tell him! When did we first meet?"

"Six months ago," she explained dutifully. "He made a pass at me in the drugstore." Sylvia laughed and then felt very lonely doing it. Chloe continued. "It's like I said before, Mr. Lockwood. I'll bet my bottom dollar Roscoe is no longer in this country. And frankly, I can't understand all the fuss about him. He's such small pickings."

Max couldn't resist the opening. "Not if he leads to solving Judge Kramer's disappearance, and other fringe benefits. Morgan Montescue doesn't think Roscoe's such small pickings. Why arrange for him to be sprung from San Quentin?"

"Poor Roscoe," said Chloe. "Nothing ever did go right for him. What a star-crossed life he's led. Well, Max, for Roscoe's sake, I hope you never find him. He deserves to spend his last years in peace."

"He won't," said Lockwood. "Not while I'm on his trail."

The Pied Piper took a healthy helping of chopped liver.

Edna saw the perplexed look on Sylvia's face and beckoned her to her side. In less than a minute, thereby breaking her own world's record, Edna had imparted to Sylvia the rest of the Roscoe Mears story. All the while Sylvia's eyes never left Chloe's face.

"Now," added Edna under her breath, "do you believe there's a book in those sisters?" Sylvia nodded slowly, and Edna smiled complacently. "I've just about convinced Max to collaborate with you."

Sylvia's heart skipped a beat. "Thank you, Edna," she whispered.

"He's also writing the preface to your book."

"My cup runneth over. I thought you didn't like Max."

"A woman's prerogative, sweetie. I have to admit, he's quite a guy." Lockwood came into her line of vision. "But there's more of that one." She turned swiftly to Chloe, who was on the verge of rising. "Chloe, Sylvia and Max want to write a book about you and your sister."

Chloe sank back into the chair and Max blushed. "We're not all that interesting," said Chloe.

(Cool, thought Max, you're very, very cool.)

(Unreal, thought Madame Vilna, these people are unreal. Why did Piper suddenly drop the fork full of chopped liver? True, for my taste there is not enough onion and chicken fat, but nevertheless . . . why?)

"Sloppy," self-admonished the Pied Piper as he dabbed at his lap with a napkin.

"Of course you're interesting!" insisted Sylvia. "Look at all the fascinating characters you used to know!"

"And," added the Pied Piper as he wiped chopped liver from the carpet, "the fascinating ones you've met the past six months."

Chloe's laugh was a tinkling one and it subsided in twenty seconds. "Wait till I tell Ramona. What a snit *this'll* bring on. Forget it, Sylvia. Ramona hasn't enjoyed one moment of the past half year."

"Not *one?*" boomed Madame Vilna.

"Not one, sorry. She wants to retreat again. I don't. So we've compromised. Mexico. And there you have it, my dears." She made it to her feet. "I better get back and see if she's all right."

Max helped Chloe into her coat as Sylvia led the way to the

door. "Now, Chloe," said Sylvia, "I want you to consider this idea carefully. There could be an awful lot of money in this. Hard cover, paperback, magazine serialization, foreign rights, movie rights, stage and television rights—and you adored that taste of the spotlight you had this afternoon."

"A taste is enough," said Chloe in the doorway. "More could be fattening."

"Still, Chloe, it's worth considering." It was the Pied Piper who spoke.

Chloe said, "Goodnight, all," thanked Sylvia and left.

"She is also not *real!*" The furniture shook and Madame Vilna reached for the bottle. "It is like when I starred as Rucheleh in *Vuss Zet Minn im Der Glayzerleh,* which is perhaps more familiar to you as *Alice in Wonderland.* It is all *unreal!*" Still clutching bottle and glass, she slumped onto the couch, her head dropped on her ample bosom, and she was asleep.

"She's passed out," announced Edna, and Sylvia proceeded to remove the old woman's shoes.

"She can spend the night here," said Sylvia. "Poor old soul. She's been in a terrible state all evening. First Ramona, then Quasimodo." She met Max's inquiring glance and repeated most of her earlier conversation with Madame Vilna.

The Pied Piper finished eating and stifled a yawn. Edna wondered if Lockwood would ask to see her home. Lockwood was wondering, as Madame Vilna had wondered, what was behind Ramona's mask . . . *"The real mask."* Max had found a comforter in the bedroom and covered Madame Vilna.

Sylvia finished talking, folded her arms and awaited reactions. No one spoke. "Don't you get it?" said Sylvia. "The poor old soul's waiting for the real *everybody* to please stand up."

The Pied Piper chuckled. "I assure you, Sylvia, I am very real. What you see is what there is. And now it's time for me to retire."

"Don't forget Simon Winkle," contributed Edna.

"Goodness, thank you. He completely slipped my mind."

"Now that you've made a killing," said Max with a benign smile, "don't let it tempt you into falling into any bad gambling habits."

"I am not easily tempted, Max." He said his goodnights, Sylvia took him to the door, and after he departed, Sylvia remained leaning against the door.

"Why must old age be so sad?" she asked the room plaintively.

"It doesn't," offered Edna. "I'm planning on a spicy one for myself. Mr. Lockwood, dare I prevail upon you to escort me home?"

"You dare indeed. Max, how's for breakfast in the morning?"

Max agreed. "Eight at my hotel."

Madame Vilna began snoring.

Alone, five minutes later, Max and Sylvia sat on the loveseat holding hands. "From the beginning, Max," said Sylvia, "I want the whole Roscoe Mears story and don't leave out a thing. Shall I make some coffee?"

"You'd better, and very strong."

At two o'clock in the morning Gypsy Marie Rachmaninoff awoke with a start. She had fallen asleep in her chair in the store. She blinked her eyes and then rubbed them. The solitary burning lamp came into focus. She raised herself and moved quietly to the room behind. She passed through the beaded drapes and looked at her son's cot. It was empty. Her hand moved to her mouth and she began to moan softly. Fear and apprehension moved her to action. She crossed to the phone and dialed. On the third ring, there was a response.

"Yes?" Sylvia was definitely annoyed.

"Sylvia, it's Gypsy Marie."

Sylvia was immediately all concern. "What's wrong?"

"He hasn't come home. Quasimodo hasn't come home. Sylvia . . . you've got to find Max and tell him." Her voice broke. "Please Sylvia, I'm desperate."

"Max!" she heard Sylvia shout. "Max, wake up! This is serious! Quasimodo is positively *missing!*"

Madame Vilna's hangover was so monumental, she contemplated laying a wreath at its base. The fizzing of the glass of Bromo Seltzer she held in her hand was nerve-shattering, the chug-a-chug of the agitated electric percolator at her elbow was like a drum solo in an echo chamber. The weather wasn't half as gray as Madame Vilna's mood. She downed the Bromo in three gulps, placed the glass on the table, and then erupted with an ear-shattering belch. She reached out her hand and found the damp towel that had been in service for the past hour, since Max had dropped her off at her house, pressed it to her throbbing temple and then lay back on the couch.

Why, she agonized to herself, why did I do it? Why did I down so much slivovitz, like a Polish general programing a pogrom? Why did I work myself into such a state over Ramona Grace and the Pied Piper? Why did I so glibly label them unreal to Sylvia and yet still probe for an authentic basis to the accusation? Somewhere in my subconscious there lies the answer, and I shall not move from this couch, from this apartment, until I find it.

Was it sun spots? What made for such a crazy yesterday? Sylvia's party. Why did I feel such a strain at the party? Age cannot wither nor fortune stale my infinite variety of suppositions. Chloe was uneasy. The Pied Piper was uneasy. Likewise Max and his delicious friend from San Francisco. Sylvia was as nervous as a turkey the week before Thanksgiving. And that Edna St. *Eppis* I could do without.

Poor Gypsy Marie. Poor distraught mother. The child. The sad little boy with the curse on his back. A runaway. Perhaps kidnapped? Who would kidnap the son of a gypsy? Only another gypsy. Why would a gypsy want to steal a deformed child? Why don't I forget gypsies and think about what's important? Who will read with me if Ramona and Chloe leave for Mexico on Saturday? Why Mexico? Why leave?

She scratched a thigh while contemplating. Life is a masquerade, she decided. Ramona's mask is real, but ours are invisible. I hide my fears, my loneliness, my occasional insecurities behind a very robust good nature. Last night was a masquerade.

Masquerade.

She sat up. She poured herself a cup of coffee and forced herself to drink it black.

Masquerade. She flung the towel aside and stared into the cup of coffee. Last night's party was miraculously reflected. She could see the guests, and she shuddered at the sight of herself downing another slivovitz. She saw Gypsy Marie sewing and Edna's knee rubbing Lockwood's and Max talking to Chloe and Sylvia digesting Max with her eyes and the Pied Piper spilling chopped liver. Why was that? Ah yes. It was coming to her. The mention of the book about Chloe and Ramona.

She set the cup aside and gently fingered her wattles. Carefully she attempted to reconstruct the previous evening. What was there about it that seemed so familiar to her? But of course! A rehearsal! She leaped to her feet and began pacing the floor with her hands clasped behind her back. We were all like actors attempting the first run-through of an extremely poor play. The direction was inadequate, the dialogue was forced, everyone was unsure of themselves and there was a poverty of honest characterization. Everyone attempted but no one succeeded in playing their role well. And whyyyyyy?

"Because," she raged at the French windows, "bad casting!"

The floor was at her mercy as she tramped back and forth with punishing tread. Bad casting! We had assigned ourselves our roles for the evening and all were ill-suited. Sylvia's gayety was a pretense. Lockwood's conviviality likewise. Edna's bluster similarly so. Gypsy Marie's serenity as she sewed was a sham. Max's calm a façade. Chloe's cool exterior was badly forced. And what was the Pied Piper attempting to convey? And I, of course, was shamefully overacting.

But I was not alone. Aha! So was the Pied Piper!

Actors. Masquerade. Masks. Costumes. Wigs.

"Dear God," she bellowed, "I think I have it!" Her voice dropped to a whisper. "I think I have it." She positioned herself at the fireplace, right hand on the mantel, left hand on her hip with fingers tapping, positively Phaedre.

Max wishes me to arrange a private tête-à-tête with Ramona Grace. Tête-à-tête it shall be. Her face brightened. At last, she thought, at last Vilna assumes a role she has never played before.

Detective.

In the back seat of the patrol car nosing its way through traffic toward Brooklyn, Max Van Larsen was grateful for Burton Lockwood's silence. Conversation at breakfast had been strained and desultory. Neither had had much sleep. Max's mind was a *paella* of mixed emotions. The case of the missing Quasimodo had been placed in the competent hands of an associate. But in whose competent hands could he place the case of Max Van Larsen?

What's wrong with myself lately? he asked himself while dreading the answers. Is it possible for a person to remain so dispassionate? Is it possible for a man to be so devoid of humility? Last year, when a boy disappeared, I was able to become involved with him and feel for him without ever knowing him, and weep at the sight of his lifeless body. Why can't I feel and become involved with the living? I know I love Sylvia Plotkin and yet my lips refuse to form the words. I have never said, "Sylvia, I love you," and she's being cheated. And I thereby cheat myself. I loathe sham, deceit and hypocrisy in others, yet I, Max Van Larsen, feel guilty on all three counts. A hunchbacked boy, a pathetic creature so desperately unhappy, takes it on the lam, and instead of commiserating with and understanding the act, I grumbled and cursed and hated his guts for robbing me of a warm bed and a warmer body. I deceive myself into thinking people charming and amusing, when in truth I find them tiresome. Last night the Pied Piper was tiresome and he irritated me. Likewise Chloe. Madame Vilna says they are unreal, and somehow I think she may be right. Am I that easily influenced by other people's opinions? I suppose so, at times. Everybody is. But perhaps that isn't the case at the moment. Did Lockwood just say "Urmph"?

He stole a glance at his companion and saw a beatific expression, with eyes as vacant as the majority of offices in a new highrise. He returned to his own thoughts.

Until yesterday and Burton Lockwood's arrival, I had no reason to examine these people carefully. The Pied Piper, Chloe and Ramona. They were there, part of the Village scene. Part of Sylvia's scene. Sylvia has a talent for collecting strays. (I, if I will admit the truth, among them.) All my life I've viewed people from a distance, from the wrong end of the telescope. Everyone tries to involve me. Why can't I learn to involve myself? Lockwood is completely involved with Roscoe Mears. He lives and breathes the man. He can even think like the man. I can't. I have never been able to. It's like Lockwood said, I'm methodical. Coldly dissociated. And therein lies the truth of my dissatisfaction. I don't enjoy my work. The people I'm assigned to find disinterest me. And if that's the case, how can I be any good as a writer?

Sylvia's book was raw and crude and amateurish, but beautiful. It was Sylvia. It was real, it was honest. Edna was clever not to alter a line of it. That's why people buy it and love it. It glows with Sylvia. When Sylvia passed on Madame Vilna's comment about me, "For Van Larsen, a handshake is passion," I guffawed. But it rang hollow and empty, like myself.

Oh, come now, Max. Don't be all *that* tough on yourself.

Lockwood stole a look at Max and wondered if he had indigestion. He'll pop a pill in his mouth, and I wish I could pop back into bed with Edna St. Thomas Shelley.

Really, Max, thought Max, you're not all *that* bad. Whether you've expressed yourself to her or not, you *have* fallen in love with Sylvia and give her a great deal of pleasure. (Humility, Max.) You give her a great deal of frustration too. I ought to take Quasimodo to the zoo or to a movie. Sylvia will have to come too. She'll be able to cope with the kid. Where the hell could he have run off to? Gypsy Marie insists he had no money. No money won't get him very far. Damn-fool kid and his damn-fool habit of snooping and looking into windows. One of these days he'll see something he shouldn't see and . . .

"What's wrong, Max?" he heard Lockwood asking.

Max turned to him. "I just had a funny notion about the Quasimodo kid. Ah, the hell with it, I'm just reaching."

"What's the notion?" Lockwood sounded genuinely interested.

"Well . . . I was wondering if the kid might have seen something last night he shouldn't have seen. That kid doesn't strike me as the type to run away."

"Kids change fast, Max."

"Maybe. But this kid wouldn't know where to run to. He'd run to *someone,* not to a place."

"Why the sudden interest?"

"I don't know. It just happened to come to me. Sylvia's so

concerned. She sat up all night with his mother."

"She's a good broad."

(She's a lady, damn it, not a *broad*. I don't traffic with broads!)

"Yes," said Max, "she's very good."

"Getting back to the kid, who would he run to?"

"The Pied Piper, I should think, but he says he hasn't seen him."

"Funny how a lot of roads seem to lead to the Pied Piper." Lockwood stared out the window for a moment and then spoke again. "He was very much on edge last night. He didn't like being caught out on the horse-playing bit, for one. I'd like to talk to that—what's his name—the bookie . . ."

"Simon Winkle."

"Winkle . . . yeah. Like to have a little chat with him. Like to know what he knows about your Pied Piper's habits. Might be interesting."

"The chat can be arranged. Winkle occasionally comes in handy to the police. That's why we don't bother him too much. I'll get on to him when we get back to the precinct."

Lockwood asked unexpectedly, "Who said 'Time is the enemy'?" Max hated non-sequiturs and hoped the expression on his face was appropriately vague. It must have been, since Lockwood continued without waiting for a response. " 'Time is the enemy,' " he repeated slowly, like a wise man addressing his disciples. "Something Chloe keeps insisting makes me think I'm misjudging Roscoe, or I've been overcomplacent thinking he'd slip up and drop into my lap just like that." He snapped his fingers in emphasis. "She says he's already left the country. I don't think he has, but I suspect he's about to. Max, she's seen Roscoe."

"If she has, we'll never get her to admit it."

(Cool, Chloe, real cool.)

"She's seen him," continued Lockwood doggedly and positively, "and it ties in with the sudden announcement that she and her sister are taking off for Mexico. A very hasty decision, Max, very hasty." His lips curled into a contented smile as he folded his hands over his stomach. "Haste makes for slip-ups. Which brings me to a long shot. Quasimodo snoops around a lot. I don't know, Max, I don't know. He just might have poked his nose yesterday a bit innocently into a situation he didn't understand, but could prove very dangerous to the person who caught him. I feel uneasy, Max."

Max leaned forward to the policeman behind the wheel. "Check the precinct and see if there's anything new on the Rachmaninoff kid, and tell them to have Simon Winkle in my office in about an hour or so."

As he leaned back, Lockwood announced, "I'm beginning to hate Henry Wadsworth Longfellow."

Max had always suspected a toss in the hay with Edna St. Thomas Shelley might be unhinging.

"He said, 'Learn to labor and to wait.' The 'wait' is all wrong, all wrong, Max."

Ilsa Brandenburg was a portly German woman in her mid-fifties who dealt in services. She was a licensed masseuse, a registered nurse, loved to march in parades carrying standards, and moonlighted twice a week as Simon Winkle's cleaning woman. His was an easy apartment to tidy, Simon being compulsively fastidious. In addition to the nominal sum he paid her (including delectable leftovers from his refrigerator), there were frequent hot tips on the horses, and all in all, the arrangement was a highly profitable one for Ilsa. It helped keep up the mortgage payments on her comfortable little house in Queens and added to the substantial contributions she made to the highly suspect Germany Awake! Society of which she was secretary-treasurer and bouncer.

She blithely hummed the "Horst Wessel Song" as she inserted her key in the lock, twisted it, heard the familiar click and entered Simon Winkle's apartment. The television set was on and Judith Crist in no uncertain terms was condemning Roger Corman's latest movie. She saw Simon Winkle's arms dangling limply over the sides of his chair and yodeled a cheery *"Guten tag!"*

Accepting no response as the little man's preoccupation with the critic's heady dissertation, she semi-goose-stepped to the closet, opened the door, removed her hat, took off her coat, and after disposing of the garments, marched to the kitchen and the broom closet. With a firm grip on a rag and a can of furniture polish, she returned to the living room and announced with train-conductor volume, "I begin today in ziss room, *mein herr!"*

Mein herr neither said anything nor changed position, and this was unusual. Simon Winkle was always chipper, cheery and chatty.

"Herr Winkle?"

She circled the chair, saw the tiny lifeless eyes, the tiny tongue protruding from the cupid's-bow lips, and the tiny scarf tightly tied around his tiny neck.

"Achtungggggg!" she shrieked, and the Jewish refugee next door paled and went hunting for the old yellow armband.

For a fleeting moment Burton Lockwood was trying to recall his last visit to a wax museum. Surely a Pygmalion must have visited Madame Tussaud's, selected Lita Swenson Kramer as his Galatea, brought her to life, transported her abroad and set her up in Brooklyn. He hadn't seen such lavish eyebrow-pencil slashes since Dietrich's heyday at Paramount. The hazelnut eyes could easily prove a challenge to a near-sighted squirrel, the orange gash that passed for a mouth must have been inspired by Picasso, and the make-up was most certainly applied by an undertaker. Were the velvet swallows in her yellow bird's-nest hair decoration or merely pausing en route to Capistrano? And who, he added to his silent inventory with a repressed shudder, uses a raisin for a nose?

"Coffee? Tea? A liqueur?" trilled Lita after ushering them into the vast living room, and Max waited for a hidden flautist to offer counterpoint. All seated, refreshments refused, the detectives entered briskly into the business at hand.

"Memories, memories, memories!" she sang, gaily waving a ten-inch blue lace handkerchief. She repeated the names Mathew Armand Kramer, Chloe Grace, Ramona Grace, Roscoe Mears, Nola Kemp (off-key) and Morgan Montescue like a lyric from "The Jewel Song." "That's all so many, many, many, many *years* ago!" She positioned her left hand palm downward under her chin and studied the two men reflectively. "I barely knew Roscoe Mears. He'd have no reason to get in touch with me."

"On the contrary," remonstrated Lockwood, "you might know how to put him in touch with Morgan Montescue and/or Nola Kemp."

"Nola *Kemp!*" The raisin quivered with rage, and Lockwood prayed it wouldn't drop at her feet. "I never knew *she* existed until *after* my husband's disappearance."

"What about Montescue?" asked Max.

"Heaven only knows," she said with a sigh.

"We know he's alive," said Lockwood, and told her of the lawyer's connection with Roscoe Mears' release from San Quentin. She listened quietly, attentively, immobile and without blinking an eyelash to Lockwood's theory that Mears was in New York to attempt to collect the missing Kramer fortune and would probably think nothing of committing murder in order to lay his hands on it. Hadn't Montescue administered Kramer's estate after his disappearance?

Lita leaned forward. "Now, Mr. Lochinvar . . ."

"Lockwood," Burton corrected politely.

"So sorry," she said mincingly. "I see everything romantically. I'm sure you're aware that shortly after Matty's disappearance I had a complete breakdown, which brought about a severe case of amnesia and caused a three-year confinement.

When"—her hands now clasped in supplication, her eyes fixed dramatically on the ceiling—"I recovered and returned to face life again on Ocean Parkway, just about everyone I had known had gone underground!" Her hands fluttered gracefully and she cocked her head winsomely, the little match girl trying to push a sale on two men who owned cigarette lighters. "That was late in thirty-five. Racketeers were scattering to the winds to escape the long arms of the government! Greece! Italy! Brazil! I'm sure that's why poor Monty ran. He knew so *much*. His greatest danger was from his *own* former associates! If Monty was found and made to talk even *today,* there are vast financial empires built on the blood money of yesteryear that would crumble!" She paused expectantly, but no applause was forthcoming. "Fortunately, much of my husband's holdings were in my name, so I'm quite comfortable. Of course," she added with a theatrical flourish, "I thought at one time of attempting through the courts to reclaim the properties he'd assigned . . . that *woman* . . . but a cooler head prevailed and I let it drop."

"Whose cooler head?" asked Max swiftly.

"My own, dear," replied Lita with a cold smile. "Lita Swenson Kramer knows when to keep her nose out of a mess."

(Surely, madame, thought Lockwood, you jest.)

Max decided on a different attack. "Do you recall the day your husband disappeared?"

"Vividly." The word whipped his ear.

"Was there anything unusual about his behavior that day, and the days preceding it?"

"Sad to say, I was too preoccupied with myself and my career in opera to pay much attention to Matty. As you well know, much went on between Matty and others of which I was totally unaware."

"He was unusually wealthy for a judge," said Lockwood.

"Not at all," parried Lita. "Good friends shrewdly guided his investments. Monty pulled him out of the market before it crashed and crushed, and then guided him back in again when top securities were going at bargain rates." She stamped a foot in irritation. "What's all this got to do with Roscoe Mears?"

"We think Roscoe knows what happened to your husband." Max thought she turned pale under the wax, but would never be sure.

"Roscoe was a nobody," she snapped.

It was an old technique, but Lockwood was positive Max would pick up his cues. Max did, and they began firing a dizzying barrage of questions.

Lockwood: "Who handles your affairs today?"

She blurted out the same law firm that represented Morgan Montescue, and Lockwood began to feel cheerful.

"How well did you know Rightie McGurk?" shot Max.

"Hardly at all!"

Lockwood: "Weren't he and Ramona lovers?"

"God, no, it was Chloe."

Max: "Who fingered your husband?"

"Don't be crude!"

Lockwood: "Wasn't he pulling double crosses all over the place? Especially Morgan Montescue?"

She jumped to her feet. "Monty says there wasn't . . ." and then her hand flew to her mouth.

"Mrs. Kramer," said Lockwood softly, "where can we reach him?"

As abruptly as she rose, she sat and began nervously twisting the handkerchief, then straightening up bravely, she piccoloed, "I find you gentlemen offensive. Please go."

Max mustered some charm with an effort. "Monty's an old and valued friend, isn't he? If Roscoe Mears finds him before we do, he just might kill him."

"Oh." She might have just been stabbed.

"Oh, indeed. There was an attempt on Roscoe's life in San Quentin. Wasn't that Montescue's doing?"

"No no no no no!" She was on her feet again and stamping her feet like an insolent child. "The last thing Monty wants is

Roscoe dead! *Oh!*" She staggered back into the chair with a stricken expression.

Max found a card in his wallet and placed it on the coffee table. "Will you ask Mr. Montescue to get in touch with me?" She stared at the card, transfixed.

The doorbell rang but she appeared not to have heard it. Max and Lockwood exchanged glances, and it was Max who crossed to the door and opened it. His driver spoke two sentences, Max whistled, then shut the door and returned to the room. He told Lockwood, "Simon Winkle's been murdered."

They heard a sound like escaping steam and turned and saw Lita Swenson Kramer slide from her chair onto the bearskin rug in a dead faint.

Gypsy Marie Rachmaninoff sat at the table behind her crystal ball, staring at the door and willing it to open and Quasimodo to enter. Sylvia Plotkin had taken a reluctant and tearful departure for Robert Wagner High School an hour earlier. Gypsy Marie's eyes moved from the door to the traitorous crystal ball and on to her trembling hands, which she was slowly raising to her tear-stained face. She sobbed for several moments as she had sobbed most of the night, as she had sobbed the day she realized she had been abandoned in her pregnancy. Then, with a sudden resolve, she pushed the chair back, lurched to her feet, grabbed the corncob pipe, fumbled for a match and lit up. Slowly, deep in thought, she circled the room like an angry lioness. One word throbbed in her mind and then came ablaze with hate.

Lies.

The word turned neon-red.

Lies.

She stared into the crystal ball. It was there too.

Lies.

The Pied Piper lies. *But why,* she asked herself again. *Why?* He lies about betting on the horses. I'm positive he lies about being at the school last night when he should have been at Sylvia Plotkin's. Then he assuredly has lied about not seeing Quasimodo last night. The Pied Piper is his only friend. It is the Pied Piper he would have run to. And if he wasn't in the basement of the school, Quasimodo would have ferreted him out. Quasimodo finds *everyone* he's looking for. He knows their every move from years of study. The boy's brain is a fantastic filing system of timetables.

The Pied Piper lies, and by God, I, Gypsy Marie Rachmaninoff, shall choke the truth out of him if necessary.

Her face softened briefly.

He has been so kind, this old man, so dear. Why should he lie, especially about Quasimodo? He has been so devoted to him, so kind, so understanding.

Resolve returned.

She reached for her shawl and drew it tightly around her shoulders. There were lots of initially kindly old men in her life who had turned out to be ruthless charlatans. Remember the motto of the tribe, "Trust No One and Wield a Big Stick." She stared around the room but there was no big stick. She stared at her strong hands.

They would suffice. She went in search of the Pied Piper.

After placing her on the couch, patting her wrists and finally forcing some brandy into her mouth, the two policemen waited until Lita Swenson Kramer revived and sat up. "What happened?" she asked weakly.

"You fainted," said Max. Lockwood handed her the swallows that had escaped the nest when she keeled over.

She wet her orange lips as she blithely tucked the birds back in place, then sat back with her arms folded. "I'm all right now, thank you. You may go." She dismissed them with a royal toss of her head that sent the bird's nest bobbing and the swallows nodding affirmatively.

"Simon Winkle," said Max.

Lita unfolded her hands and let them drop to her side. "I'll have Monty call you," she said with a tired voice. "That's all I can do for you now. You have to believe that. I know absolutely nothing about my husband's disappearance. I know nothing about Roscoe Mears or why he would want to kill Monty or anyone. Monty and Roscoe want Nola Kemp for two different reasons. But it's up to Monty to explain that. Monty will be in touch with me. I promise I'll make him call you. Please go. I have to practice. *Mi Fa So Do Mi La Sooooo!*" she suddenly cadenzaed, the startled Lockwood almost leaping into Max's arms.

"Was Simon Winkle mixed up with Montescue?" Max persisted.

"I said *gooooo!*"

Lockwood grabbed Max's sleeve and led him outside. In the street, Lockwood said with a pleasant smile, "Longfellow's back in my good graces. He's absolutely right. 'Learn to labor and to wait.' There was no use pushing her any further. The lady was undoubtedly instructed to lead us a merry chase. She got winded in the home stretch. Montescue will contact us. Let's get back to civilization."

The elevator in Lily's house deposited her in the basement. She rushed into the soundproof studio and confronted the octogenarian cripple in the wheelchair.

"Ah, my dear! Rid of them so soon?"

She ignored the question. "I want the truth, Monty. The truth, you hear? Did you order my husband's death?"

CHAPTER X

The heaviness in Sylvia Plotkin's heart was proving to be an unbearable weight. After her tear-drenched farewell to Gypsy Marie Rachmaninoff, she was beset by the gnawing hunger that always found her vulnerable when she was depressed and frustrated. She entered a luncheonette, found a vacant stool and glumly ordered coffee and a buttered bagel. While waiting to be served she examined her face in her compact mirror, grimaced, and patted her cheeks with powder. Lipstick would be a waste until after she'd eaten. She snapped the compact shut, dropped it back into her purse, closed the purse and propped it on her lap.

Her thoughts were blacker than the fingernails of the truck driver on her right.

The success of the book has made me smug and complacent and I'm not the darling I used to be. True, it is a major accomplishment, but did Edison lose his humility after inventing the electric bulb? When I cried most of the night with Gypsy Marie, was I crying for the missing boy or for myself? What can come of this relationship with Max? There I go again. I should be thinking of Quasimodo, not Max.

I've known Max longer. He wins by seniority.

You'll never marry me, will you, Max? The wounds of your miserable union with your deceased wife still fester and might never heal. I fill a certain need in your life, but with you, certain needs rarely ripen and mature. I have never heard you say, 'I love you, Sylvia,' and Max, man does not live by bread alone. You held me in your arms last night, but I had the feeling it was with the weary resolve Gargantua must have felt when he settled for Toto. I wonder what's become of Toto. I understand you, Toto. I honestly do, woman to woman. I, too, wander restlessly within the confines of a cage. The bars are invisible, but they exist.

So if not Max, who? (Whom?) Some teacher.

"Sell what you can, you are not for all markets." Shakespeare by way of Edna St. Thomas Shelley. (Did you make out last night, Edna darling? May you live and be well and this morning purchase a mute for the brass instrument that passes for your mouth.)

Collaborate with Max. Preface by Max. The preface I'm living now, the collaboration I would adore, but not just on paper.

She stared down at the cup of piping hot coffee and the two halves of buttered bagel. She hadn't noticed them placed there. She sipped the coffee and wondered if it had been strained through a flyswatter.

I have been depressed before, but this is absurd. I should be reveling in my celebrity! Why not? I earned it. Nobody gave it to me. Why am I so protective about *his* feelings? Why do I continue deferring to him? Why do I humble myself in his presence? Am *I* not *also* a catch?

But of course, you stupid woman! You are a catch! You're a good schoolteacher, a successful author, reasonably attractive, highly affluent, a bit on the dumpy side, but concentrated dieting can correct that.

She took another sip of coffee.

All right, so concentrated dieting won't correct it. A sylph I'll never be, a sylph I never was—and how many sylphs have written best sellers? Willa Cather was a sylph?

It's settled. I'll have it out with Max. As soon as he and Burton Lockwood have found Roscoe Mears, I'll have it out with Max. And supposing I have it out and I'm left with it? Oh *hell!* In the words of a very great Southern philosopher, *Fiddle-dee-dee, I'll think about it tomorrow.*

Now why was the party such a bomb? Why did everybody seem so phony, including yours truly? True, the reunion with Max was a bit of a strain, but with Max, what isn't? And Madame Vilna gulping slivovitz like it was going out of style. She started it. That's it. All that nonsense about Ramona and Piper being unreal. Piper bet on a horse. Well, why shouldn't he? Don't I buy lottery tickets? That's different. It's for a worthy cause. But Piper betting on a horse is completely out of character. Completely out of *what* character? Such a dichotomy. (Thank *you,* David Susskind, wherever you are.) But there are two sides to everybody. Breathes there a man or woman who isn't Janus-faced? Well, answer me, Sylvia. Breathes there? Piper, Ramona, yes, and Chloe. That was a very different Chloe last night. Very different.

What was that strange remark she passed at Schrafft's yesterday. Something like *it's never too late to make amends, is it, to one's self that is.* Is Mexico amends? And how come all of a sudden?

She pushed the bagel aside and lit a cigarette, and tried to review the facts of the Roscoe Mears case as told to her the previous night by Max.

Chloe and Roscoe. Ramona, Chloe and Roscoe. Ramona, Chloe, Roscoe and Judge Kramer. And Nola Kemp. And Morgan somebody. Quasimodo. Why do I suddenly include that poor unfortunate in this group? Because they're all poor unfortunates. They are Greek tragedy, though none of them is Greek.

(How do I know that? What do I know about, for instance, the Pied Piper? Very, very little. Very little indeed. Unusual for me. You're slipping, Plotkin.)

What made Lockwood think Piper might have been in New York years ago and known Roscoe Mears? It isn't impossible. He said himself he was a wandering troubadour, and wandering troubadours cover a lot of territory. It could also give them corns and bunions, but that's why there's darling Dr. Scholl. Wouldn't it be funny if Piper knew Chloe and Ramona when they were young and beautiful? If he did, why keep it a secret? After all, it was he who won Chloe over and got her out of that musty old reconverted church and . . .

I feel so cold all of a sudden. Why is that? It's very warm and cozy in here and I couldn't possibly eat that bagel now because I've lost my appetite because the gnawing hunger has given way to my gnawing intuition and by God I'm going to have a talk with Piper *right now*. He's been lying to me damn it and nobody lies to Sylvia Plotkin because she doesn't like kindness repaid with lies. (Is that why you are kind, Sylvia? For payment?) Nonsense! He's been lying and lying is lying. He was very *noodgy* last night about the horse betting and fixing the pipe in the basement last night and Simon Winkle finding him out and he's the logical person Quasimodo would have run to after the rumpus with Madame Vilna.

What am I doing to him all of a sudden? Who am I to place him in the hot seat? He's a dear and a darling and the children adore him and *I, said the Demon.*

But that's neither here nor there. Rasputin liked children too . . . raw, probably. I'll never rest until I get all this out of my system. Never. Quasimodo might not have run away at all. He might have snooped himself into trouble. I'll bring Gypsy Marie some chicken soup later. Can chicken soup replace a child? No, but by me it's penicillin.

"My check, please," she cried to the counterman and rouged her lips with two professionally deft strokes.

. . .

"Hell," groaned Chloe at the window, partially hidden by the heavy drapes, "it's Madame Vilna at the door." She folded her arms and turned her back. "Maybe she'll go away."

"Madame Vilna never goes away," was the irritated reply, the voice harsh and husky. "Go talk to her, I'll be out in a minute. I'll settle her."

"You're so sure."

"I'm *very* sure."

"How do your hands feel? Are the bandages too tight?"

"They're just dandy."

"Stop *snapping* at me. You need a fresh surgical mask. This one's filthy."

"Will you for crying out loud go talk to Vilna! She'll break the door down!"

Madame Vilna's shako, hastily grabbed and plopped on her head when she rushed from her apartment, was decidedly ill-suited to the majestic purple velvet opera cape in which she now snuggled, but then, she thought to herself as she attacked the door knocker again, this is a period of incongruities.

"Chloe! Ramona!" she shouted at the door impatiently. "It is *Vilna* speaking!"

The door opened and Chloe stood on the threshold with a fixed smile on her face. "Aren't you the early bird!"

"Good morning, my dear Chloe. Is your sister up and about?"

"She's up and she'll be about in a minute. She's still a little shaky on her feet after yesterday's indisposition. I just put fresh bandages on her hands. I suppose you've come to bug her about the reading."

"It is not a matter to be treated lightly," said Madame Vilna sternly. "Can you so easily dismiss our great tradition of the theater? The show must go on!" Her hand shot up and shook the shako. "Do you invite me in or must I stand trembling on your doorstep like an Avon saleswoman?"

"Of course. Come in."

Madame Vilna did not cotton to the note of reluctance, but she was a woman with a mission, and no mission in Vilna's life ever remained unfulfilled. She barged past Chloe into the sitting room and stationed herself in front of the blazing fire warming her hands. "Mexico will be very pleasant at this time of the year."

"We hope so."

"I toured there many years ago. They adored me as Chanah in *Bluterdicker Chassanah,* which perhaps you might recall as *Blood Wedding.* I played it for laughs. At a dinner in my honor the president of the republic, whose name escapes me since his deposement, drank tequila from my slipper, which proved to be singularly unfortunate as it was open-toed. Now then, what keeps Ramona?"

"Good morning."

The harshness of the voice grated on Vilna's ears and she turned. "Good morning, my dear Ramona. I offer my solicitations for your painful mishap. You sound very irregular this morning."

"I'm not well."

"I wonder, my dear Chloe, would you find it offensive if I was to converse, as your dear Mexicans would say, *solamente* with your sister?"

"She's all yours. I have something to do upstairs."

As Chloe left, Madame Vilna sat in an easy chair, indicating the sofa to Ramona. Ramona chose a straight-backed chair and sat stiffly.

"I suppose there is no convincing you to postpone your trip until after the reading?"

"I'm sorry. No."

"You leave me stranded very high and dry, my dear, and it is massively a disappointment. However, I have more strings to my fiddle and am already considering pressing our dear Sylvia Plotkin as your substitute. You are suppressing a professional giggle?"

"No, dear. I'm sure Sylvia will do fine."

Vilna rummaged in her bag for a Turkish cigarette, and as she did, she carefully studied the bandaged hands, the ill-fitting dress, the surgical mask, the vivid blue hair, and then locked eyes with Ramona. "Van Larsen has asked me to arrange a private tête-à-tête with you."

"Whatever for?"

Madame Vilna blew a smoke ring before replying. "Perhaps he has romantic inclinations! Ooooh wah ha ha ha ha ha!" It took thirty seconds for her robust laughter to subside. "Undoubtedly, of course, in reference to the fugitive."

"He could have phoned."

Vilna's eyes twinkled. "He knows I am more persuasive. Perhaps later this afternoon at my apartment?"

"I'm sorry. I have nothing further to tell him."

Madame Vilna leaned forward with an effort. "My dear Ramona. You are very strange this morning. I understand you are a bit beneath the weather, but I have considered us friends. You treat me with such coldness now, and this disquiets me."

"I don't mean to. I didn't sleep well last night."

"Ah yes," said Madame Vilna softly, "it was a sleepless night for many people. You have heard perhaps the boy Quasimodo is missing?"

"Oh?"

"Oh. He is now the subject of an alarm."

"How sad for his mother."

"Indeed."

Ramona shifted nervously, and Vilna kept repeating to herself *unreal unreal unreal.* "Why are you frightened, Ramona?"

"Frightened? I'm not frightened."

"You are frightened and your sister is frightened. That is why you are running away."

"Really, Vilna!"

"Ah! Indignation stirs you. That is the Ramona I know. How your eyes blaze! You fear this Roscoe person and I say you are wrong. What is unseen is always most ominous. Just as what is hidden is always most attractive. The imagination can be most deceiving. For example, I find myself trying to create *my* Ramona, Ramona as I envision you behind your mask. I do not see scars."

"They're there."

Madame Vilna waved her quiet. "It is the same with the Pied Piper. I try to envision what is behind the beard. Ooooh wah ha ha! Perhaps also scars! In a sense, Ramona, is not life a perpetual masquerade? For example"—she settled back and made herself comfortable—"last night at Sylvia's unexpectedly grim gathering, I had the feeling we were all actors in an incredibly poor melodrama. I am sure Chloe imparted to you fully the details."

Ramona nodded.

"But there also comes the moment, my dear Ramona, when it is time to cease the masquerade. See Van Larsen. Help him. Even now he is in Brooklyn seeing the Kramer widow. Trust Max. He will protect you from this Roscoe person."

"I'll think it over."

"Ah! A light in the wilderness!" She struggled to her feet. "I will now leave you to rest and to think, and perchance"—she trumpeted—"to dream! I will show myself to the door." Passing Ramona on her way out, she paused to look into her eyes again and then smiled. "For a moment, my dear, I thought I saw your soul."

As Madame Vilna shut the door behind her, Ramona rushed into the hallway and shouted up the stairs, "Chloe! Chloe, come down here!" Chloe appeared and descended slowly, gripping the banister. "We've got to stop horsing around and get down to it," Ramona said. "The bastards are closing in!"

Why is there never a taxi in this God-forsaken neighborhood? Madame Vilna thought with impatient indignation. My feet feel like lead. They will never carry me to Max's precinct. There is of course the telephone, but what I have to tell him, I must tell him in person. He will perhaps think me mad, but I am not! I am not! There are masquerades and there are masquerades, but one must be more than merely clever when camouflaging for Vilna. I came in search of an answer and received a bonus. But if *Ramona* suspects what I suspicion? *Pfah!* It is not possible. I performed with admirable charm and restraint. But I have possibly stirred up a hornet's nest, and if I do not beware, I will feel the sting. *Ramona* may hazard a guess that my comment about seeing her soul in her eyes was a clever improvisation. I came to find one thing, and discovered something else. God, am I a detective!

Sylvia Plotkin hurried down the stairs to the basement of Robert Wagner High School. She heard the first-period bell and decided her gangsters could look after themselves for the opening ten minutes of the session. She pushed open the door and hurried past the furnace to the Pied Piper's room. As she reached for the doorknob, it opened.

"The Pied Piper is gone," said Gypsy Marie Rachmaninoff.

Sylvia wasn't sure which was more startling—the sight of Gypsy Marie or the information.

"What do you mean gone?"

"Gone. *Defected.*"

Sylvia rushed past her into the room. The hooks where the Pied Piper's meager wardrobe usually hung were bare. The drawers of the chest were half open and empty. His few mementos were missing.

"But . . . but . . . it's unbelievable!" gasped Sylvia. "His books are gone . . . and . . . and the chairs are overturned. And . . . look . . . the make-up box for the children's plays . . . overturned . . . everything scattered on the floor. Gypsy Marie, it looks like there was a terrible ruckus in here!"

"Or just a display of anger?" She stood with her hands on her hips, her eyes cobra slits.

"Anger? Anger at *what*? He was so jolly last night . . . he . . ."

"A façade! Sylvia, you are an innocent. I predicted dark

clouds, did I not? Your dark cloud hovers! The Pied Piper has stolen my child!"

"Oh, nonsense!" The Pied Piper in the role of kidnaper was as incongruous to her as his sudden disappearance.

"Nonsense? Nonsense? Why nonsense? He will train him for the circus! He will turn him into an acrobatic freak! How often has he filled the boy's head with such nonsense. It was Quasimodo's dream to go off with the Pied Piper." Her eyes filled with tears. "All this—" her hand sweeping the room in a deprecating gesture—"is ridiculous! He wishes us to suspect there has been foul play! He always overdramatized! I suspect he has gypsy blood!"

"I'm going to Max," announced Sylvia. "And don't you dare spread that nonsense about a kidnaping. It's no such thing! One thing has nothing to do with the other."

"I'm going with you. And if I don't receive satisfaction, I shall send for the tribe. Beware a gypsy's *revenge!*"

Sylvia shivered, grabbed Gypsy Marie's hand and rushed her from the room.

Lita Swenson Kramer was still not satisfied. Montescue had convinced her he had had nothing to do with Judge Kramer's disappearance, but she was still not satisfied. Simon Winkle had been murdered, and that could mean only one thing as far as she was concerned. He had somehow managed to find Roscoe Mears, and Mears had killed him before he could tell Montescue.

The octogenarian angrily slammed his fists down on the arms of the wheelchair. "You're behaving like a silly soubrette!"

"I'm *not!*" she squeaked. "Roscoe might have found out from Simon where to find you!"

"Never!" stormed Montescue. "Simon would never betray me. He'd sooner die, which he did, than betray me. He was like a son. I found him fifteen years ago and made him my protégé. I rescued him from sample cases and swatches and gave him position and affluence."

"Has it occurred to you, my dear," said Lita, in a rare moment of rational thinking, "that Simon's apartment might have been searched and a clue to your whereabouts found?" The old man's shoulders sagged. "I thought not. You know Simon, with his records and lists and . . . and that book he was writing! My God! Do you supose it's auto*biograph*ical?"

"My dear . . . my dear." He shook his head sadly. "We are indeed caught on the horns of a dilemma. I'm an old man, of course, and quite ready to die, but I loathe being rushed. I would so love the joy of consummating one last magnificent deal. And now I squirm under the probing of Fate's fickle finger. Come sit at my feet."

"The floor's cold."

"Take a pillow from the piano bench."

Finally, with her settled at his feet, the old man stroked her cheek. "Lita . . . Lita, love of my life . . . precious companion and devoted lover . . ."

"Yes," she whispered.

"The jig's up. If only I could have found Nola Kemp."

"I hope Roscoe's found her!" she cried. "I hope he tortures the hell out of her! I hope he kills her! Kills her! Kills her!"

"Perhaps he has and perhaps he will. You realize that if I place myself in Van Larsen's hands, all your dreams must be dismissed."

"I know," she said with a sniffle.

"Many graves will be opened and the stench will be unbearable."

"It always is with retribution."

After a brief interlude in which he was lost in thought, he suddenly wondered aloud, "Is it possible I could strike a bargain with Roscoe Mears?"

Lita brightened. "How? Is it possible?"

"By telling him the truth. By cutting him in. Forming an alliance and finding Nola together. Nosing her out of the ground, like pigs unearthing truffles. Then, perhaps, through his intervention, the Grace Sisters' church could be included in the parcel. It's all so greedy but so beautiful."

"You said yourself Ramona would never sell."

"Women, my dear, have been known to change their minds. I wish I had Barney Classon here."

"What for?"

"So I could wring his neck. Letting Roscoe slip away. In the old days . . . bah! The past can never be reclaimed. And Roscoe hates my guts. He knows I tipped Rightie about him and his affair with Chloe. He thinks I fingered him in San Quentin, but there my hands are clean. There's something else to consider. There was an item in the *Times* about the city contemplating buying up the property surrounding Ramona's. She might have seen it. She was always a very clever long-stemmed beauty. Very clever indeed. So aloof. So distant. So careful. Never an involvement. That was unusual too, don't you think?"

"She probably did have one but was too smart to let anyone find out. But somebody must have found out something, why else was she cut up?"

"I have often wondered. Well, my dear. What do we do? Lay ourselves open to Roscoe in hopes a truce can be arranged, or turn myself over to Van Larsen in protective custody?"

"I don't know. I can't think." She struggled to her knees. "I have a marvelous idea. I'll get the ouija board!"

Mama, Mama, what's taking you so long?

I hear screams. Terrible screams. I'm afraid. I'm afraid. Sometimes the house shakes. It's old. The walls are cracked. There's busted pipes. Find me, Mama. I won't ever leave you. I won't join a circus. I'll stay with you always.

She's screaming again, Mama! She's screaming again!

The house is shaking! The walls are cracking! And I hear the bell!

I'm concentrating on you again, Mama. I'm concentrating hard. Please! Please, Mama! Tune in!

. . .

Marianne Kahane flustered and fluttered around her living room like a ruffled parakeet. How dare that woman do that to me! How dare she phone and blithely announce she is canceling the City Committee for Saturday! Mexico indeed! There is a landmark to be preserved. We of the Historical Society have fought bravely and valiantly, though where others shed blood, we so frequently shed tears. There is so little beauty and tradition left in this world. In this era of ugliness, one tiny flame glows as a beacon for beauty and tradition. *My* flame. Spunky little *me*. I will not accept this cavalier attitude. It's settled! I will go and confront Chloe Grace. Oh, that strange woman, that strange sister. Of course, I might anger them and be ordered from the house, perhaps even bodily. Goodness. Heaven preserve me.

"But I must find him immediately!" shouted Madame Vilna at the indifferent desk sergeant, her shako now a reasonable facsimile of the Tower of Pisa. Her index finger seesawed under his fine Sicilian nose. "I demand you contact Van Larsen *maintenant!* Tell him it is Vilna calling, and when Vilna calls, it is *urgent.*"

"What do you want from me, lady? He's on a case, right? He's been out in Brooklyn, right? Where he goes after Brooklyn, I don't know. I told you that, right?"

Madame Vilna continued bristling. "I find you vastly inadequate. There is a radio in his car"—leaning forward with a wicked leer—"*right*? Send him an SOS!"

"Madame Vilna!"

Vilna turned and saw Sylvia hurrying toward her with Gypsy Marie Rachmaninoff. "Sylvia!" she shouted as one hand deftly readjusted the shako. "I am drowning in a sea of anarchy!"

Sylvia went past her to the desk sergeant. "Tell Max Van Larsen I have to see him at once. The name is Plotkin."

The desk sergeant wearily repeated the bulletin on Max.

"Well, find him!" insisted Sylvia. "I have *terrible* news."

The desk sergeant slowly relayed a message to the radio room.

"What is wrong?" Madame Vilna asked Sylvia with concern.

Sylvia was choking up, but finally found a semblance of a voice. "It's the Pied Piper." Vilna gently raised an eyebrow. "He's missing. Disappeared. Gone. His room's a shambles."

Vilna lowered the eyebrow and raised the other.

"Say something," pleaded Sylvia, "Piper is *missing*."

Vilna considered for a moment, and then spoke. "My dear Sylvia. You must treasure this moment. You will someday look back upon it as one of historical importance. Vilna is at last speechless."

C H A P T E R **XI**

Simon Winkle's widow fit no preconceived notion of what she should look like. Audrey Winkle, when she entered her late husband's apartment in the wake of Max and Lockwood, almost succeeded in eliciting wolf whistles. She was tall, close to five-eight according to Max's calculation. Her hair was red and boyishly cropped. Her figure seemed hand-carved, and her blue shift, which reached just five inches above her knees, did little to conceal her physical assets. Her first words upon entering alerted the boys that here was no lady to be trifled with: "Did you find a will?"

In response to their alternatingly astonished, perplexed and amused looks (Detective Herb Roper of Max's precinct, Lockwood and Max in that order), she introduced herself briskly. "I'm Audrey Winkle. My ex's housekeeper phoned me he'd gone to heaven. The sonofabitch probably has, if it's on American Express."

She sat in the chair from which her husband's body had been removed half an hour earlier, opened her purse, fastened a cigarette to a holder, lit it, crossed her legs, right over left, and jiggled the right impatiently.

"According to the laws of the state, if there's no will, it all goes to me." She waved her left hand at them, and no one could miss the thin gold wedding band. "I was never divorced, just abandoned, and I have a perfectly dreamy lawyer."

"When'd you last see your husband alive?" asked Roper.

"Three weeks ago at his mother's wedding." She inwardly delighted at the reactions of the three men she assumed to be detectives. "Dolly's eighty-two. She married her sixth. Simon inherited all his energy from Dolly. How'd he die?"

"Strangled," said Roper.

Audrey snapped her fingers. "Shucks. Somebody else always gets to realize most of my ambitions." She then asked with relish, "Did it look like he suffered?"

Max shuddered involuntarily.

Roper was speaking. "No need to tell you, I suppose, your husband was involved in a lot of shady dealings."

"No need indeed."

"Any idea who might have done this?"

"The line forms on the right."

"Did you know much about his affairs?"

"If you mean women, I know up to here," she said, indicating her neck. "If you mean where he got his income, take your pick of anything dirty, underhanded and illegal. Simon was a rat. He left me fifteen years ago after a trip to Florida. He was just an ambitious garment-center shnook then, but I loved him." She coughed briefly, and dabbed at her eyes. "I frequently choke on that line but I'm not a very good liar. I loved him. I stood alone in that class. Just about everybody else loathed him, so why didn't they throw me some hints before and up to marching down that aisle? Oh well. Water under the bridge.

"He'd probably still be cutting velvet if it wasn't for that Madame Tussaud-type opera singer and her crippled boyfriend he befriended at the track."

Max and Lockwood exchanged glances.

"Lita Swenson Kramer," contributed Max.

"Right!" corroborated Audrey with another brisk snap of the fingers.

"The crippled man," continued Max, "Morgan Montescue?"

"I can't help you there," replied Audrey. "In what few conversations we had after that meeting, he was always referred to as that smart old cripple. It was Lita who held center stage at the time. The little rat was having an affair with her."

Now it was Lockwood who shuddered inwardly.

"You have to understand something about the late unlamented that I wish I had understood at the time and earlier—Simon and adultery were synonymous. He'd lay anything and everything, which I soon realized didn't say very much for me, but I've done my own talking ever since."

"He left you for Lita Kramer." Max appreciated Roper's not interfering with his line of questioning. They had worked together too often before when a missing-person case had crossed tracks with a murder, and frequently one solution had led to the second.

"He left me for what the old cripple offered. I gathered the guy was some kind of racketeer, and Simon seemed a likely prospect for his operation. I must admit I didn't put up much of a fight when Simon took leave. I was really very, very tired at the time and anxious to get on with the business of living. After that, I can't tell you much about Simon. He was never much for confiding in anyone. He even kept bathing a secret. But he did keep diaries. He was a frustrated writer."

Max and Lockwood winced in unison.

"Keep looking, boys," said Audrey with the voice of a high school cheerleader, "they're bound to turn up."

"Some have," Roper now interjected, "but there are pages torn out."

Audrey shrugged. "Simon wouldn't like that. He had a passion for continuity. Where's the body? The morgue?" Roper nodded. "Simon wouldn't like that either. He had a passion for warm climates. For the sake of the kids, I'm claiming him and burying him. They didn't know him too well, but you know kids, they miss a father."

Max knew the pang in his chest wasn't heartburn.

Audrey got to her feet abruptly. "Unless there's anything else, I'd like to go now. For some stupid goddamned reason, I have this terrible urge to cry." She fled from the room without waiting to be dismissed.

In the awkward silence that followed, Max picked up the notebook he'd been studying when the widow had entered. He cleared his throat. "Interesting notation here," he said, and Lockwood and Roper crossed to him. Max placed his finger under one of Simon Winkle's last entries. It read: "Solon's Girl, Pied Piper, Fifty."

"Solon's Girl," said Lockwood. "Interesting. Brings to mind Judge Kramer and Nola, doesn't it?"

A radio patrolman entered. "Max."

Max turned in the direction of the voice.

"I've got three messages for you. Call Gypsy Marie Rachmaninoff, Madame Vilna and Sylvia Plotkin. All urgent."

A sly grin crept across Roper's face. "I never dreamt you and Simon Winkle had anything in common."

Okay okay okay. And one for good measure. Okay.

Quasimodo had succeeded in prying open the lock to the steamer trunk after several hours of diligent effort. Midway in his labor the muffled screams had subsided, and most of his fear had now translated into anger. He would open the trunk and the suitcases and tear up everything, that'll show 'em.

Beads. Jewels. Wigs. Dresses. Costumes. Shoes. Pictures. Very old pictures. One picture was awarded a very low, obscene whistle. It was of two long-legged beauties wearing scanty costumes.

Okay okay *okay!*

Quasimodo rummaged further. More pictures. Men. Young men. Middle-aged men. Studio portraits and snapshots. Handsome men. Distinguished men. And letters. A pack of letters carefully wrapped in blue ribbon. The boy tore at the ribbon until it broke, then opened the top letter and began reading.

Wow! Okay okay and wow! Better than looking in windows. Wow!

Max Van Larsen, thought Sylvia with impatience, irritation and more than a touch of anger as she stared at the television set with blind eyes, supposing I happened to be dying. Just suppose, Max. Just suppose. Would you ever recover from the tragedy of missing my last immortal words? Her train of thought jumped the track as she settled back cozily in the Morris chair.

What would my dying words be? "Remember me to Max." Banal.

Her eyes left the television and concentrated on the ceiling. "Tell Max I loved him to the very end." But why immortalize Max? Two hours ago I demanded that the desk sergeant get in touch with him—so where is he? Quasimodo missing. The Pied Piper missing. Perhaps Max is also missing. How often have I told him to get lost—does he have to choose today to take me seriously?

Why was Madame Vilna so anxious to get rid of me and Gypsy Marie when we left the station house? If I know Vilna— and now Sylvia's eyes returned to the television screen and the antique movie musical that must have been filmed at least thirty-five years ago—I know Vilna very well. She's up to something. She knows something and she's saving it for Max. *That's* why she got rid of us. That's it!

Sylvia leaped to her feet and began pacing the room, arms akimbo. Vilna knows something she wouldn't share because she's probably afraid big-mouth me would blab it to the wrong people. Sylvia stopped dead in her tracks. Okay. I'm improving.

I said it myself. Big-mouth me would blab. She considered phoning Vilna and wheedling whatever she might know out of her.

You can't wheedle Vilna.

But what could she possibly know? Sylvia was back in the chair. Was it something she heard here last night? Drunk as she was, it's still a possibility. She was near-frantic at the station house about reaching Max. She said she'd been to see Ramona to talk her out of Mexico long enough to do the reading Saturday night. Was it something Ramona might have said? Or Chloe? Damn it! What has Vilna found out that's so urgent? If it was something to do with Quasimodo, she would have shared it. The Pied Piper? But she didn't know then he was missing and . . . what was that I just heard? *What was that?*

Sylvia's eyes were glued to the television set. "My God," she said aloud. "Oh my God. It can't be. It can't. What the hell's the name of this movie?" She began riffling *TV Guide,* found the listing and then emitted the inimitable Plotkin scream. *"Maxxxx!"*

Although in another era Sylvia's scream might have alerted London to an air raid, it was not of sufficient volume to reach Max's ears. He was now staring with disbelief at the radio patrolman who had followed his initial message with the news of the Pied Piper's disappearance.

"Jesus wept," whispered Lockwood hoarsely. "There's a lot of that going around these days."

"How long missing?" Max asked the patrolman.

"Miss Plotkin reported it two hours ago. She and the Rachmaninoff broad checked his quarters at the school. The place was in a shambles and the bed hadn't been slept in."

Lockwood leaned against a wall and studied Max. In less than twenty-four hours' acquaintance, he had come to admire and respect him. He had even begun to understand and appreciate the man's seemingly constant stoicism. But now a veil dropped from Max's face. He was visibly distressed by the news about the Pied Piper. Lockwood felt better. Here at last was a sign of the third dimension he'd been looking for in Max, a third dimension Sylvia Plotkin must have found back in the dark ages when she first met him. He knew it had to be there. Why else would someone as warm and outgoing as Sylvia Plotkin fall for the Dutchman?

Herb Roper's voice broke the silence. "Think there's a connection with Winkle's murder and Quasimodo's disappearance?"

"There has to be," said Max in a voice they didn't recognize. "I'm convinced the kid saw something that got him into trouble. Maybe Piper tracked the kid down and landed in the same spot . . . and somehow it has to tie to Winkle."

"And Roscoe Mears." Lockwood had shifted position and now stood with his hands in his pockets, staring at the floor. He looked up abruptly and spoke to Max. "We've got to force Morgan Montescue into the open. We can't wait on Lita Kramer. We've got to smoke him out of his hole fast and let Roscoe Mears find him. Let's bring in Lita. That ought to make Montescue come out and cast his shadow, predicting, I'm sure, foul weather."

Max gave the instructions to the radio patrolman, who nodded and left. Max crossed to the phone and dialed.

Marianne Kahane shut the gate to the old church resolutely, tucked a stray strand of hair back under her hat, shifted her bag from her right arm to her left, then marched with a military bearing up the path, the ten stone steps, and attacked the bell with her index finger.

Mexico indeed, she bristled to herself. There's sorry little charm left in New York. There's sorry little charm left in the world—but the world was somebody else's territory, and from what she read in the daily newspapers, they were welcome to it. Here and there in this city there are tiny oases, reminders of a past and by far better world, and they needed to be *preserved*. If only for the sake of our children and *their* children, to be reminded that ours is a heritage to be looked back on with pride. Look what's happened to the Grange—Alexander Hamilton's magnificent home near City College fallen into sorrowful disrepair, with no funds available to restore it. Look what they're doing to the stately homes of Staten Island. And how soon before they remove the ferry?

Even the Astor Hotel gone! She'd had her first date under that lovely old clock in the lobby. Next thing you know, they'll be razing Fraunces' Tavern and the old Trinity Church! Everything going to make way for cold, lifeless, antiseptic superstructures.

She attacked the bell again.

"Miss Grace!" she shouted at the door. "Miss Grace! It's Marianne Kahane! I must *talk* to you! Miss *Grace!*"

"Miss *Grace!*"

Chloe flattened herself against the bedroom wall, moved the drapes slightly and stared down at the intruder. She muttered an epithet under her breath and then crossed to the bed and resumed her packing.

"Miss Grace! It's Marianne *Kahane! Please* talk to me!"

Chloe scowled. Talk. Everyone wants to talk. Everyone except the one we *need* to talk. Filthy, stubborn bitch. Filthy . . .

Chloe had flung open the door. She crossed to the stairs leading to the bell tower and took them two at a time. Reaching a solid oak door, she extracted a key from her pocket and entered the room. The bound and gagged figure lying on the bed stared at Chloe with defiant eyes.

Chloe shut the door and leaned against it. "The money, you bitch, the money." She crossed slowly to the bed. "Where's the *money?*"

The eyes closed as Chloe's fist connected with a cheek.

"The *money!* Tell me! The *money!*"

"Miss *Grace!*"

Marianne Kahane stepped back and stared at the upstairs windows. Determined, she said to herself, that's what I am, determined. She walked down two steps and sat. I shall sit here all day if necessary. All day! She decided to try one for good measure.

"Miss *Grace!*"

"Miss *Grace!*"

Quasimodo climbed atop the steamer trunk and peered anxiously out the barred window.

I know that voice. Okay okay okay. That crazy lady who sometimes gives Mama jams and jellies. Kumquats. *Eeeyich.* Orange marmalade not bad. Okay okay okay.

"Hey, lady!" he shouted, but "Hey, lady!" met another "Miss *Grace!*" in mid air, collided and shattered.

Chloe pulled the oak door shut behind her, locked it, and clutching the key, descended the stairs. She entered her bedroom and crossed to the window. She looked out cautiously. Damn! Kahane's still there. I've got to get rid of . . .

And then something fluttered past the window toward the ground. And then another something. Chloe caught a glimpse of the third something.

My God. It's *me*. An old photo of *me*. Oh God! The kid's throwing them from his cell. He's broken into the steamer trunk. They're fluttering down toward Kahane.

Chloe sprinted toward the hall.

One photo landed in a bush several yards from Miss Kahane's vision, swept there by an uncooperative breeze. The second photo landed on the path, but Miss Kahane had swiveled her head to stare at the door irately. The third photo landed in her lap. It rested there unseen for some thirty seconds until Miss Kahane repositioned her head.

"Goodness me," said a surprised Miss Kahane in a Little Miss Muffet voice. "And where did *this* come from?" She picked the picture up gingerly with thumb and index finger and saw only a blur. With a sigh of exasperation she placed the photo to one side and rummaged in her bag for her spectacles.

As she adjusted the eyeglasses to her face, the door behind her opened slowly.

Miss Kahane reached for the photo, but connected instead with a foot standing on it. She looked up abruptly.

"Why, Miss Kahane," said Chloe Grace, "how *long* have you been sitting *here?*"

Max dialed Sylvia's number again, but there was still no reply. He slammed the phone down and addressed Lockwood. "Let's take a look at Piper's place." As Lockwood nodded, Max spoke to Roper. "If you come across anything you think we might use, I'll be back at the precinct in about an hour."

Lita Swenson Kramer peered cautiously out the window at the weird apparition who'd been worrying her chimes for the past minute.

"So?" hissed Morgan Montescue. "Who is it?"

Lita turned to him. "It isn't a *who,* it's a *what.*" She'd arpeggioed the information but flatted on the last word. "The most outlandish creature!"

"Is today Hallowe'en?"

"How would I know?" asked Lita grandly. "You know for me time has no meaning."

The chimes reverberated again.

"Describe this creature," said Montescue with monumental patience.

Lita positioned herself against the fireplace, Tosca about to attack an aria. "It's a woman," she said slowly and mysteriously, "a very large woman."

"Go on, go on!"

"She's wearing a Queen Mary hat with a veil that comes down to her nose." She slowly moved away from the fireplace and began circling the wheelchair, fingers stroking her waxed chin. "Her hair is a very garish blue. I think it's a wig." Montescue's head shot up as Lita continued. "Oddly enough, she's wearing some sort of surgical mask obscuring the lower portion of her face. Her right hand is in a large fur muff. A very ratty fur muff, like the one Ruth Etting carried when she sang 'Ten Cents a Dance' in the *Follies of 1931*. Her left hand's completely bandaged."

"Ruth Etting?"

"The thing on the doorstep."

"Silly goose. Don't you realize who it is?" He cackled gleefully. "It's Ramona . . ."

". . . *Grace?*" The bird's nest quivered.

"Let her in! Let her in!" Montescue cried eagerly. "It's providence, I tell you, providence! She can lead us to Roscoe Mears! Quick! Quick! Let her in! Let her in!"

He prodded Lita's backside with one of his crutches, and after a swipe at the instrument with her left hand, Lita went to the door and opened it.

"Ramona Grace," said Lita darkly, "I never thought you'd dare attempt to cross my threshold *ever.*"

A bandaged hand came full across Lita's face, and with a maniacal shove, sent her sprawling backward to the floor. The front door was kicked shut, and Morgan Montescue, eyes blazing with fear, feebly waved the crutch.

The second bandaged hand emerged from the ratty fur muff, brandishing a section of lead pipe.

"Ramona! Ramona! You're crazy! You're crazy! We can help each other! *Ramona!*" cried Montescue. "Put that down! *Ramona!*"

C H A P T E R **XII**

Gypsy Marie Rachmaninoff cautiously raised the door of the wire-meshed cage in the backyard behind her store. She reached in, took a firm grip on the pigeon, and then very carefully inserted the small wad of paper in the capsule attached to one of the pigeon's feet. Then she held the pigeon's head close to her mouth and whispered fiercely, "Find my tribe! Deliver this message! I need them!" She raised her hand above her head, relaxed her grip and released the pigeon. It soared above her, then reversed and came swooping low over her head. Gypsy Marie ducked as she snarled, "None of that. Just deliver the message." The pigeon dipped a wing in a graceful salute and soon disappeared over the roof of an adjoining tenement.

Gypsy Marie folded her arms and returned to the store. She crossed the living quarters, through the beaded curtains, and settled in a chair at the table. She unfolded her arms, passed her hands swiftly over the crystal ball and then breathed a sigh of relief.

"Thank God. He has good flying weather."

· · ·

Madame Vilna sat alone in the women's section of her local synagogue, a black lace shawl over her bowed head. Her tightly clasped hands rested in her lap, the piercing eyes now shielded by shuttered lids. Her lips moved in a silent prayer. A few minutes later she whispered "Amen," opened her eyes, unclasped her hands, grasped the railing in front of her and pulled herself to her feet.

I am cor-*rect,* she said to herself, I know I am positively cor-*rect.*

Eyes do not lie. Eyes cannot *poss*-ibly lie, hence, Vilna is cor-*rect.*

But do I dare a confrontation alone and without protection? Should I perhaps, after all, confide in darling Sylvia Plotkin? Or should I once again seek out darling Max Van Larsen?

She sighed a very dramatic sigh and leaned against the railing, pondering the dilemma.

Alone, with Sylvia, or with Max?

As she struggled for the decision, her eyes slowly panned around the interior of the house of worship.

For shame, Vilna, for shame. How infrequently you come here. How infrequently any of *us* come here. So much for assimilation. When was the last time I heard the ram's horn blown? How long has it been since I honored the Day of Atonement? Why does old age make so many of us aware of religion? Is it to make peace, or an apology? Even Vilna the atheist had cried out for God on his deathbed after a solid season of cursing Him for a disastrous tour of *Der Meshuganeh Boychik,* which audiences soon recognized as *Hamlet.* Vilna, she thought to herself sadly, you were the best of all my husbands, but on your deathbed, did you have to disappoint me with a display of hypocrisy? Or had the atheism been the hypocrisy?

Alone, with Sylvia, or with Max?

Max.

She slammed a fist against the railing and edged her way with difficulty to the aisle.

Max, eyes do not lie.

Gypsy Marie's pigeon took a breather on the head of one of the lions in front of the Fifth Avenue public library. He'd been bucking a strong headwind all the way up from Greenwich Village. From the lion's twin there wafted toward him a sultry, seductive "Coo." He cocked his head.

"Coo." It was a subtle invitation and she had the face of a nightingale.

"Coo" again.

Damn, thought the pigeon, I've been weeks cooped up in that cage, and opportunity would knock in the middle of an assignment.

"Cooooo."

Steady, he said to himself, steady. Stronger birds than I have been defeathered by invitations like this. Steady and away. He took wing and soared past the hen, dipping his wing in remorse. Bravely he flew into the wind, his instinct guiding him to the New Jersey side of the George Washington Bridge.

Impatiently tapping one foot, Sylvia Plotkin sat on a bench staring at the desk sergeant. He stared at the tapping foot.

"Miss Plotkin," he said with a measured degree of patience. "If Van Larsen is anywhere near a radio car, he'll get your message."

"This is *very* unlike him," insisted Sylvia with the authority of one who'd made a complete study of the detective's habits. "He's usually very *good* about checking in with the precinct."

"I told you, he checked in an hour ago. He doesn't check in every hour on the hour like a cuckoo clock."

"You're *sure* he knows the Pied Piper's missing?"

A man studying the wanted posters on the bulletin board thought the desk sergeant deserved a medal for the patience with which he was handling the nut case. The Pied Piper's missing. Next there'll be a red alert for Pinocchio.

"Yes, Miss Plotkin, I'm sure."

"And there's been absolutely *nothing* on *Quasimodo?*"

The man at the bulletin board winced and stole a quick glance at Sylvia. For crying out loud, he thought to himself. I think I saw that broad on TV last night. She's the one who broke down in tears at the end of the program. Well, whaddya know. She really did crack. Success does that to a lot of them.

"Nothing. Not a lead. Be patient, Miss Plotkin. We'll hear from Max."

Oh yes, we'll hear from Max. Sooner or later everybody hears from Max. Why doesn't anybody ever hear from Max when one needs to hear from him *desperately?* And I, Sylvia Plotkin, teacher, authoress, lover, in no particular order of importance, need to hear from him *now*. I possess vital information. *Very* vital information. And there it goes again. I'm hearing it again. It's like a broken record. It sticks in my mind and keeps repeating and repeating like the Chinese water torture.

I, said the Demon!

The pigeon followed the George Washington Bridge across the Hudson River and paused for a moment on the window ledge of a motel room. As it gasped for breath, it stared through the window into the room and gulped. So *that's* what goes on in these places. Heavens. He took off, wings flapping as though motor-propelled, and let his homing instincts guide him. Then to himself he whispered "Eureka!" as he sighted about half a mile ahead of him toward the Palisades a circle of canvas-covered wagons. The tribe!

"Christ! It's a blood bath!"

The two radio-car patrolmen had found the door to Lita Swenson Kramer's house ajar. In the center of the huge living room was an old man slumped at the foot of a wheelchair, head brutally bludgeoned, still clutching a crutch with his right hand. Staring past him, they could see a woman lying on the fireplace hearth, wig askew, also bludgeoned. The officers crossed to the old man, and one knelt at his side.

"This one's wiped out."

They hurried past the dead old man to the woman.

"I'll be damned," said the first officer huskily, "she's still breathing. Her lips are moving. She's trying to say something." He lowered his head, bringing his left ear to her mouth.

"What's she saying?" asked the second officer anxiously.

The first officer waved him quiet as he screwed up his face straining to hear the dying woman's words. He caught something and repeated it to his colleague. "Sounds like . . . Galleecurchee . . . something like that." The second officer shrugged as the first strained to hear what followed Galleecurchee. "This one's clearer. Sounds like . . . Martini . . . or Martinelli."

"Maybe she wants a drink."

"Wait a minute. Now she said . . . Ramona."

"Ramona?"

"Yeah. You know. Like in 'I hear the mission bells above.' "

He continued straining for several moments, then shook his head in defeat. "She's had it. Get the word to Van Larsen."

The ten-year-old gypsy boy aimed his air rifle at the pigeon circling above the camp, but the pigeon kept darting and swooping frantically, making a sighting difficult.

"Attila!"

The boy recognized the shriek. He turned to see his mother running toward him from their wagon.

"Attila! Don't shoot that bird! Haven't you been taught to tell the difference between an eating pigeon and a homing pigeon?"

The boy stared at her with his usual vacant look.

"That's a homing pigeon!" she shouted. "He knows us. Can't you tell? Honest to God, this family's cursed. Gypsy Marie and her hunchback, Lupescu and her one-armed flamenco dancer and a lot of good those castanets do him, and me, Zsa-Zsa, with a dolt like you!" She grabbed the gun from his hands and smote him brutally on his backside. The boy was too stupid even to rub where it hurt.

Zsa-Zsa shielded her eyes against the strong sun with her hands as she made cooing noises. "Come here, my lovely, come here!" By now she was surrounded by other members of the tribe.

"It's exhausted, the poor thing," cackled an elderly Rom.

"Of course it's exhausted," agreed Zsa-Zsa. "Look at the poor thing. He's a special delivery."

She stretched a hand out palm upward, and the weary bird soon settled there. Swiftly the capsule was emptied and the note read.

"It's Gypsy Marie!" shrieked Zsa-Zsa as the pidgeon hid its head under a wing. "Quasimodo's been stolen!"

"Quasimodo's been stolen!"

"Quasimodo's been stolen!"

"Quasimodo's been stolen!"

Ionesco, the gypsy chief, pushed his way to Zsa-Zsa's side. "Let me see that message!" he said in a voice of thunder.

"What for?" challenged Zsa-Zsa. "You know you can't read."

Ionesco gave a moment's contemplation to belting her one in the mouth, but the defiance in her face alerted him to a possible swift retaliatory kick in the groin. Zsa-Zsa had always been a fast girl on her feet.

"Hitch the wagons!" he bellowed to the crowd. "And set your compasses for Greenwich Village!"

Campfires were doused, belongings were piled into the rears of wagons, and horses were hitched. Zsa-Zsa, holding firmly to the reins with her right hand and brandishing a whip in her left, shouted to Attila, "You stupid boy! Are you getting into the wagon or do you prefer to be left behind?"

The boy shifted from one foot to the other.

"Well?" shrieked Zsa-Zsa.

The boy said sweetly, "I'm thinking."

. . .

Sylvia's backside felt numb, but her brain was as nimble as ever. Why did Gypsy Marie suspect the Pied Piper of kidnaping Quasimodo? What reason would the old man have for stealing the boy? Show business? If so, how long do you disguise a hunchbacked child, especially if it's appearing before the public?

Nonsense. Quasimodo had no special talent, although one had to admit he'd refined snooping to a fine art.

Snooping. It has to be that. Quasimodo saw something, something the Pied Piper did.

Oh, Piper, Piper.

She groaned inwardly.

Have I been wrong about you? Did the Plotkin radar finally fail me? Are you a monster and not a man? But you adore children and they worship you, none as steadfastly as Quasimodo. Could you betray someone who loves you? Were you ever betrayed by one who loved *you?* Is that it? Is it?

I think it is.

Sylvia shifted on the bench, crossed a leg, positioned an elbow on her knee and propped her head with a fist.

I, said the Demon!

I've got to think this out carefully. Very carefully. I'm on to something, not because I'm positive but because I trust my instincts. And where were your instincts, darling, when you trusted the Pied Piper? Oh, you hush up, you suspicious little devil I inherited from my mother's side of the family. Now I must think like a Steinhaus (maiden name).

Betrayed. That's the key word. Betrayed. Who betrayed who and why? Betrayed. Yes, I must start there.

"Doesn't make sense," said Max to Lockwood as they examined the Pied Piper's room. "It looks to me as though he took it on the lam. All his personal belongings are gone."

"Know much about this school?" Lockwood asked from out

of left field. He was seated at the table, sorting through a small carton.

"Only what Sylvia tells me. It's a school like any other city school." He had joined Lockwood at the table.

"They put on a lot of shows here?"

"Graduations . . . Christmas . . . Thanksgiving . . . that sort of thing."

"Then they'd need more make-up than this sorry collection." He held up the carton. "Look inside. Spirit gum . . . a couple of jars of base . . . some funny noses . . ."

"Yes," agreed Max, "they'd certainly need more than this." He held up the tube of spirit gum.

"Read the label pasted on the other side."

Max turned the tube over and read the label. He emitted a low whistle. "This tube's traveled a long way."

"So have I, Max, so have I. This bloodhound's at the rear . . . and nipping. We're getting close, Max. We're getting very close. Close to Roscoe Mears and Simon Winkle's murderer."

"Max!" The voice came from the doorway. The two detectives turned as the radio-car officer entered. The veins in Max's temple throbbed as he heard of the brutal murders of Morgan Montescue and Lita Swenson Kramer. He nodded solemnly as the officer repeated Lita's dying words: *Galleecurchee . . . Martini . . . Martinelli . . . Ramona . . .*

"Ramona," repeated Max.

"And, Max," said the officer, "Sylvia Plotkin's waiting at the precinct to see you."

"Okay," said Max. "Okay."

The officer left the room.

"Max," said Lockwood after a moment's thought, "we've got a maniac on our hands."

"Burton," said Max, "to use a very familiar lyric—I think we better get us to that church on time. There are too many flights to Mexico to suit me."

"Halt!"

In the doorway stood Madame Vilna, one beefy arm raised like Moses commanding the Red Sea to part.

"How fortunate I wended my way past this public in-stee-too-shun and saw the police cars. And where there are police cars, I say to myself, Madame Vilna, there could very well be Max Van Larsen. Where have you been *hiding?*" she growled.

"Please, Vilna," implored Max, attempting to push past her, "I've no time to talk now."

Vilna was immovable.

"You *must* listen to me, Max. You positively *must!* I must tell you about the *eyes!*"

Lockwood's shoulders slumped.

"Eyes!" cried Max. "I can't talk about eyes now. I've got to get to the church. To Chloe and Ramona."

"Aha!" the old woman shouted triumphantly. "We are two great minds sharing one thought. *Those* are the *eyes* I must discuss with you. Now listen to Vilna, do you hear, or I shall make mountains *tremble!*"

When Marianne Kahane followed Chloe Grace into the house, she felt a certain uneasiness. She'd felt nothing like it since the time in a darkened hallway when she'd nearly been raped by a drunken janitor. There was something frightening in the way Chloe had taken her foot off the photo on the stoop and very slowly torn it into tiny pieces, scattering it to the winds like an irresponsible litterbug. Prudence had cautioned Miss Kahane to refrain from any comment at the time. As she followed Chloe, she found herself babbling nervously.

"Surely, Miss Grace, you know what a terrible state of disrepair this building is in. There's the underground stream once used for transporting runaway slaves eroding away the foundations. When you permitted me to have the house examined, we were warned the walls needed shoring up, and what's more, the bell tower sways. So you see, you can't possibly leave for Mexico before the Historical Society sees the house. Why, it could come tumbling down around your head any moment! Now you wouldn't like *that,* would you? Why are you staring at me so strangely, Miss Grace? Is it something I said? Miss Grace . . . Miss Grace . . . put that andiron down. Oh, Miss Grace . . . you *mustn't. . . !"*

"I've got it!" shouted Sylvia as she leaped to her feet, the desk sergeant almost tipping over backward in his chair. "By God, I think I've got it! Listen, you! When Max checks in, if he ever checks in, tell him Sylvia Plotkin's at the old church. Do you hear me? I've gone to the old church to see Ramona and Chloe! Write that down. Ramona and Chloe."

The desk sergeant dutifully took notes as Sylvia scurried for the door.

"And tell him to hurry!" shouted Sylvia over her left shoulder. "As I am about to tread where angels fear, and if I know Sylvia Plotkin, she might very soon be in danger!"

C H A P T E R **XIII**

In her cubbyhole of an office, Edna St. Thomas Shelley sat rocking gently in the swivel chair behind her desk, one hand gently stroking the manuscript of *Parole Officer* by Burton Lockwood (and for a moment she thought she heard the gentle murmur of an "urmph"), the other hand gently flicking ash in a tray gifted to her by an innocent author in a rash moment of generosity. (Someone had kidded him into believing that when an advance is subtracted from royalties, there's a balance.)

Parole Officer.

The son of a gun really can write. It was raw, it was crude and the spelling was atrocious, but it was completely engrossing. She'd have to work very closely with Burton on the revisions. As closely as they had worked most of the previous night, she thought with a delicious grin, though nothing then required any revision.

A heavy wind began rattling her windows, and she turned to stare outside. "Damn," she muttered. A storm coming up and no umbrella or raincoat for protection. I wonder if I can make it to the Graces' before the storm breaks.

Fifteen minutes earlier she had come to one of those momentous Edna St. Thomas Shelley decisions that had made her so invaluable to the publishing house. She was positive there was a good book in the Grace Sisters, and she intended to nail them down to a commitment and hand it to Sylvia on—she giggled—a Sylvia platter.

She would arrive at the reconverted church unannounced, storm the barricades if required, and fast-talk the old ladies into a deal. She knew how to handle old ladies. Didn't her list of mystery authors read like an advertisement for Medicare?

The Sisters Grace. Two sad, tired old ladies. Strange, thought Edna, how old age can wrap a cloak of dignity around a pair of tramps.

Put the kettle on, girls, here comes Edna.

There's a storm coming, Mama. A terrible storm. The wind sounds like a bunch of angry lions. No, Mama, I never seen an angry lion, but you know Quasimodo, I got a good imagination. And this place is beginning to rock and the bell is clanging like crazy and I can hear it just as loud even if I cover my ears with my hands and I'm afraid, Mama, I'm afraid. Real fierce I'm afraid.

Can't you tune me in, Mama? I been concentrating on you real hard. Don't you want me back, Mama? Don't you miss me like I miss you? Concentrate on me, Mama. Wish me back. I'll be good. I won't look in windows no more. I'll clean the pigeon coop and do my homework and flush the toilet when I'm finished. I'll be a good changeling, Mama, honest I will. You said I should learn to tell the truth, Mama, and I'm real smart and I'm learning, so I'm telling the truth.

I'm afraid.

I'm alone and I don't like storms and there are two new cracks in the walls, and if you're not here, how can I crawl into bed beside you and you hold me tight until the storm goes away to Connecticut like you always say it'll go.

I threw pictures out to the jelly lady, hoping she'd look up and see my hand waving out the window, but something must have gone wrong. I tried yelling, but she didn't hear me because she was yelling herself and the wind was strong.

Mama. I got bad news for you, Mama. I think they're gonna kill me, Mama. I do. I really do. So please, Mama, *please,* tune in, tune in. I'm *concentrating.* I'm concentrating real *hard.*

Please, Mama.

I know I'm not a nymph, so why am I being chased by a satyr? And goodness me, he's playing a flute or a similar form of wind instrument. He's getting closer. Ah yes, it's pipes. Goodness me, it's Pan! The tune's familiar too.

Myyyyy des-ert is *wait*-iiiiing . . .

Goodness me, that's a real oldie. I just wonder. It's been *so* long. Should I let him catch me? Goodness me, the very thought of *that* has given me a headache. Oh, how my head aches. Oh oh oh. What agony. What agony. My head, my head.

With a drawn-out moan of pain, Marianne Kahane's eyes fluttered open. Frequently given to cliché, she accordingly whispered, "Where am I?" The pain behind her left ear was excruciating and her fingers gently explored the area, coming away stained with blood.

Miss Grace.

Miss Grace! She propped herself up with difficulty on an elbow. I was struck with an andiron by Miss Grace! Why, that beastly woman! *That's* the kind of thanks I get for trying to preserve her homestead.

The look on her face. I'll never forget the look on her face. I saw a look like that just once before in my life. Olivia de Havilland in *The Snake Pit.* Ghastly. Hideous. Unsporting. How dare Chloe Grace strike defenseless me. And *why?*

"Miss *Grace!*"

That's not my voice at all. If it is, I sound perfectly dreadful. She sank back. What am I lying on? Where, indeed, am I?

Slowly she blinked her eyes to force them into focus. That's obviously a ceiling. A very old, very cracked ceiling. And unless my ears deceive (which well they might, I've been deceived by so much lately), I hear the gentle lapping of water. Perhaps I've been set adrift in a canoe. But I feel no gentle motion. And I don't hear Hiram plunking away at his banjo and singing "Oh, You Beautiful Doll." My mind's wandering, and this is no time for errancy.

With renewed effort she propped herself up again on her elbow and stared at her surroundings.

Goodness me, I'm in some sort of cell, and somehow I have the feeling I have been here before.

I have!

It's one of the subterranean cells in the old church, where they hid slaves!

She pushed herself into a sitting position with her feet hanging over the cot.

My feet are getting wet, and these are a new pair of Enna Jettick shoes.

She stared down at her feet.

"Water!" shrieked Miss Kahane.

The cell is flooding with water!

"Miss Grace! Miss *Grace!*" she cried hysterically. "The cell is flooding! It's pouring in from a crack in the wall! Miss Grace, save me! I can't swim! I shall drown! Miss Grace! *Please,* please save me!"

Sylvia Plotkin bravely fought the buffeting winds as she rounded the corner into the street that led to the old church. It's a hurricane. It has to be a hurricane. If it has to be a hurricane, does it have to be today? And if it's positively a hurricane, how come it wasn't predicted last night by Uncle Weathby?

The clanging of the old bell was near-deafening and the street was deserted. Sylvia found refuge in the doorway of an abandoned building to catch her breath.

What I am doing is sheer insanity. It has to be sheer insanity, otherwise it wouldn't be Plotkin. Max will kill me for this. I know he will. Why am I so rash? This could be suicide. Am I a teacher and an authoress and a lover, or a Kamikaze pilot?

I am a determined woman. I have been trained to deal in facts and I must know the facts. If I have been betrayed, I want an explanation. I am owed that. I should have waited for Max. I'm tired of waiting for Max. Why is my hand shaking? My hand is shaking because I am frightened. If I am frightened, why don't I go back to the precinct and wait for Max? Because I'm tired of waiting for Max and I am also very stubborn and impatient. And I have this subconscious desire just once in our relationship to beat Max Van Larsen to an answer.

A ferocious gust of wind sent an empty ashcan rolling past her, the sudden clatter breaking her train of thought. She looked across the street at the old church and could have sworn she saw the bell tower swaying. Maybe that bell's clanging for help. The noise is frightening. The silent street is frightening.

A cab draw up at the church and with a sense of relief she saw a familiar figure step out.

"Edna!" she shouted, emerging from the doorway at a difficult trot. "Edna!"

As the cab pulled away, Edna St. Thomas Shelley lowered her head like a charging bull and managed to make it to the gate.

"Edna!"

Edna, thought Edna. Well, it's my name. One hand shielding her face against the brutal wind, she turned and saw Sylvia Plotkin, purse clutched to bosom, fighting through the wind toward her.

"Sylvia?" Edna cried with surprise, the wind almost forcing the name back in her mouth. "Is that *you*, Sylvia?"

"Who were you expecting?" gasped Sylvia as she finally reached Edna. "Storm Jameson? What are *you* doing here?"

"At the moment," shouted Edna, "I'm thinking of lashing

myself to this gate. I hope the old girls are at home. We need refuge."

"Edna," said Sylvia, her mouth now pressed to Edna's ear, "it may not be much of a sanctuary in there. I think I'm on to something about those women and the Pied Piper, and I think it's something terrible and dangerous."

Nature couldn't equal or surpass the hurricane of words that flowed from Sylvia's lips in the following two minutes, punctuated every two or three sentences by Edna's "No!" or "It can't be!" and occasionally "Well, I'll be damned."

"So what do we do?" asked Sylvia at the end of her breathless discourse. "Do we go back and find Max or do we go in? I mean, I'm game if you are and what's more . . ."

Into her line of vision past Edna's head came a familiar figure heading for the church. "We're trapped."

Edna turned and followed Sylvia's look. "Who is it?"

"Ramona Grace."

Edna saw the blue wig, the Queen Mary hat, the veil and the muff, and commented drily, "She must be the pretty one."

"Miss Grace! Miss *Grace!* The water is almost up to my knees! Oh, Miss Grace, Miss Grace . . ."

Marianne Kahane's voice faded into silent despair as another torrent appeared, this time streaming from her eyes. I mustn't cry. I really mustn't. Surely there's a way out of this. What did Alice in Wonderland do when she almost drowned in the sea of her own tears? Didn't she find a piece of cake labeled "Eat me"? Miss Kahane frantically looked around the cell, but there wasn't a piece of pastry in sight.

This can't be happening to me! It can't be! I was meant to die in bed, clutching a lily in my hand. How dare I be treated this way! Man's inhumanity to man. Shocking. Disgusting. Beneath contempt.

Without realizing it, Miss Kahane had sloshed her way to the cell door. She grabbed the knob and began rattling it wildly with all her strength, all the while shouting, "Miss Grace! Miss *Grace!*"

A prayer on his lips and the stick in his hand, the helicopter traffic-surveying pilot guided his frail craft through the onrushing hurricane toward the East River heliport. Passing over Seventh Avenue in the Village, he looked down and saw a hopeless traffic jam. With one hand he rubbed his eyes. It wasn't possible. Is that a wagon train down there, three abreast, with the wind tearing at the canvas tops? The traffic was backed up for at least ten city blocks and he could well imagine the accompanying cacophony of automobile horns and cursing drivers. With a sigh and a fresh prayer, he radioed the situation to base.

"Can't you get us out of here?" pleaded Max to the young officer behind the wheel.

"Max," said the driver wearily, "it'll take an airlift to get us out of here."

The wind howled about the car, and Madame Vilna, squeezed between Max and Lockwood, drew her shawl tighter around her shoulders. *"This,"* she said, *"this* is a *storm!"*

Lockwood gently patted the old woman's knee in reassurance and was astonished at being rewarded with a broad wink.

"For crying out loud," yelled Max, "don't just sit there! Get out and see what's holding us up!"

The driver opened his door, slid from behind the wheel and clambered upon a fender, the wind almost succeeding in sweeping his cap off his head.

"Of all times to be caught in a traffic jam," said Max as he rubbed his sweaty palms on his trousers. "I'll kill Sylvia," he added, "I'll kill her." A check to the precinct had brought the information that Sylvia was on her way to confront the Grace Sisters. Madame Vilna patted one of his hands. The driver stuck his head in the car.

"Gypsies," he said.

Max stared at him in disbelief. "What about gypsies?"

"A whole goddamn caravan of them up ahead jamming the street. Some of the boys are trying to break it up, but from here it don't look easy."

Max left the car to see for himself. Half a block up ahead, concentrated in the area fronting Gypsy Marie Rachmaninoff's establishment, was a tight cluster of at least a dozen gypsy wagons. The noise of the wind was no match for the noise of the automobile horns. Litter flew in all directions and the sky was blanketed with a heavy gray.

"I'll be right back!" shouted Max into the car.

"A pox on you!" Gypsy Marie shrieked at four bewildered policemen.

"A curse on both your houses!" screamed Zsa-Zsa.

"The evil eye will pursue your children!" Ionesco shouted.

"What the hell's going on here!" It was Max elbowing his way toward Gypsy Marie.

"Van Larsen! At last!" cried Gypsy Marie. "This is my tribe," she informed him with great pride. "They have come to help find Quasimodo."

"Get them out of here!" shouted Max against the wind. "You've got me bottled up back there. Sylvia may be in trouble. Come on, Gyp; get them moving."

"Sylvia? Trouble? This has something to do with Quasimodo?"

"Yes! Now for crying out loud get them out of here!"

"Where, Van Larsen? Where?" She was clutching at his lapels.

"The old church. Now get them out of here!"

"The old church!" She turned to her family and shouted, "To the old church!"

"What old church?" asked Ionesco in a rare rational moment.

"Follow Marie," cried Gypsy Marie as she rushed to the lead

wagon, clambered aboard, took a firm grip on the reins and bellowed, "Giddyap, you Cossacks!"

I feel okay okay okay. I don't know why, but I feel okay okay okay. Mama must be coming. I know it. I feel it. Shut up, you crazy bell! You're making the place shake. Shut up, I tell you! Look! Another crack in the ceiling. Oh my oh my oh my! It's coming apart. The whole place is coming apart.

Hurry, Mama, hurry! Remember that crazy story you told me about the temple of the Philistines? Same thing here.

Hurry!

This situation, thought Sylvia Plotkin with a sinking sensation in the pit of her stomach, is a nightmare. What was it Madame Vilna kept insisting last night?

Unreal!

"This is unreal!" exclaimed Sylvia.

"But it's what's happening, baby," she heard Edna from behind her.

"Really, Ramona . . . really, Chloe," said Sylvia nervously as she and Edna were being backed toward the staircase leading to the bell tower. "You very kindly invite us in for a cup of tea, and then you brandish a weapon at us!" She eyed the lead pipe held by the bandaged hand with a genuine-for-Plotkin fear. "I mean . . . is this the way you repay a confidence? I reveal my suspicions about the Pied Piper, and you threaten us? But we're your *friends!*"

"Upstairs."

Sylvia stared at Ramona. It was only one word Ramona spoke, but it was harsh and ugly and menacing.

"Upstairs, and be quick about it."

Edna had already backed onto the first step and clutched at the banister to keep from tripping backward.

Sylvia continued speaking. "This will get you nowhere, you know. What I know, Max knows." (Did I sound brave and convincing? *Does* Max know? Where are you, my hero?)

"He won't find us," said Chloe. "We'll be out of here in five minutes."

Ramona jerked her head and looked at Chloe. The thin lips were parted in a Mona Lisa smile.

"I got it out of her," said Chloe. "I know where the money is . . . and she's gone stark raving mad. It's in the cellar. In one of the cells." She emitted a dry laugh. "I've got the Kahane dame locked up in it!"

"What the hell . . ." said the strangled voice from behind the surgical mask.

"It's been a busy afternoon," said Chloe. "Now go on, you two harpies. Upstairs!"

"Harpies indeed!" snapped Edna with a sudden surge of bravery. "If ever it's a case of the pot calling the kettle black!"

"Shut up and climb!" snarled Chloe. "We've waited thirty-five stinking years for this. Thirty-five miserable stinking years. Thirty-five years of imprisonment with that rotten Ramona!"

That rotten Ramona. Sylvia's eyes moved from the lead pipe to the surgical mask to the blue wig to the Queen Mary hat and to the veil. "Ramona," said Sylvia in her best Welcome-to-Open-School-Week voice, "how can you permit your sister to talk about you this way? I mean, if you're going to hit *anybody* with that lead pipe . . ."

"Sylvia," interrupted Edna with unusual calm, "what stands before you is obviously not Ramona Grace."

"Hmmmm?" hmmm'd Sylvia with a backward glance at Edna.

"Not Ramona Grace," repeated Edna evenly.

Sylvia's eyes returned to the two people menacing her and Edna. "It isn't?" she said in what she would later recall was a Minnie Mouse squeak.

They are unreal! she could hear Vilna booming.

"Of course," said Sylvia, "of course. There was something like this in the old movie I saw this afternoon." The house and Sylvia shuddered in unison and she suddenly scampered up three steps and grabbed Edna's hand, the two of them staring at their adversaries like the Gish Sisters in *Orphans of the Storm*.

Sylvia's voice was choked when she spoke. "It's you, isn't it? It's you! You betrayed me! I was your friend, I helped you!" She stamped her foot in a sudden burst of outrage. "What have you done with Quasimodo, you terrible man? You terrible, terrible man!"

A bandaged hand pulled the Queen Mary hat, the blue wig and the surgical mask away and flung them to the floor.

"Use your head," said the now-gentle voice, "use your head. Go upstairs to the tower and neither one of you will be hurt. Someday, Sylvia, someday you'll understand."

"Are you so sure? Will I really understand someday, Piper?"

Is it the wind that's howling, thought Ramona Grace, or is it me? She lay face down on the cot, mouth no longer gagged, hands and feet no longer bound.

I'm not howling, I'm singing. I always sing to myself when I'm troubled. They may have imprisoned me in this cell, but I'm the one who shot the bolt. Clever little minx. Armand used to call me that. But not clever enough, Armand. I've been outwitted.

It *is* the wind howling and the house is shaking and even I am trembling a bit. My body aches and there are probably terrible welts on my skin, but I have no mirror in which to examine them. What's another scar or two to me.

She laughed ruefully, and with an effort, rolled over on her back and sat up, staring at the dust-covered floor.

"I'm not the one who's mad. It's Chloe. Chloe, the raving maniac who destroyed my beauty with acid. It was I who defaced my soul. It was Chloe who disfigured my face. I should have killed her then. But I needed her. I didn't think we'd end up sharing our self-made prison for thirty-five years. But we did, and there's no longer a need to pay lip service to the past. The past is dead and soon I shall join it. The money. The stupid ridiculous unusable money. Greedy girl, that's what I was, that's what I am, a greedy girl. I wanted to be somebody. I was tired of sewing my own dresses and sleeping around. I was determined to give up my hemming and whoring and become somebody. I became somebody all right. A lonely, disfigured old lady soon to die.

Who's doing that yelling?

She lifted her head and stared at the door.

The kid, probably.

"Shut up, kid!" she shouted at the door. "Shut up and I'll sing for you!" With an effort she got to her feet and shuffled to the door. "Shut up, kid, and I'll sing to you! *Ol' man riverrrrr . . . !*"

Sylvia Plotkin tightly embraced the sobbing boy as Edna loudly cursed the clanging bell. Above the din she shouted to Sylvia, "I'm going deaf!" She covered her ears with her hands and sagged against the wall, watching Sylvia comforting Quasimodo.

"Quasi darling," said Sylvia into the boy's ear, "we'll be out of here soon, I promise you. Then," she began trilling through the clamor, "we'll look back on this as our one big adventure and we'll laugh and laugh and laugh." She choked back a sob.

Edna crossed to the door and began yelling through a crack, "Let us out of here, you fiends! Is this any way to treat an editor? Let us out!" She gave the door an angry kick and howled in pain. "Oh my God! I forgot they're open-toed!" There was a sickening noise as another rift appeared in a wall. The throbbing toe now took a back seat to a throbbing fear. "Sylvia!" she yelled. "Sylvia! There's another crack in the wall! The damn church is coming down around us!" She backed up against the door as Sylvia and the boy turned to look at the wall.

This can't be happening to me, thought Edna. This absolutely cannot be happening to me. Trapped by a couple of murdering maniacs. Locked up in a cell with dizzy Plotkin and a frightened hunchbacked boy. The walls tumbling down, and now I think I hear some damned fool singing "Old Man River."

"Sylvia!" she shouted. "I think I hear somebody singing!"

Sylvia replied wearily, "If it's 'Kol Nidre,' I'll listen."

"Cut through Mott Street," Max sharply commanded the driver. "We'll beat that crazy wagon train there."

Additional squad cars had been ordered to the old church by radio, in addition to a cordon to be set up around the block that encompassed the building.

"The *eyes!*"

Max looked at Vilna's strong profile with renewed admiration. What a shrewd old doll.

"*My* Ramona has *gray* eyes! The Ramona I spoke to this morning had *blue* eyes!"

Blue eyes. Pied Piper blue. Unreal. Unreal. Masquerade. Masquerade. Plotkin. Plotkin. Max's palms were wet again. If they've harmed one hair of my Juliet's head. And the boy. What if they've killed the boy? There'll be a massacre. A gypsy massacre. A pox on both your houses. A pox on one house in particular. A thirty-five-year-long pox.

Three murders. Winkle. Morgan Montescue. (An assumption the old man was Montescue but probably a good one.) Lita Kramer. Nothing disparate about that trio. All linked to each other. All linked to Roscoe Mears. All linked to the Pied Piper. That's the pattern that Max had found time to devise in his mind, and Lockwood agreed the pattern had to work. If Piper had been masquerading as Ramona, then probably there's a fourth corpse to add to the list. Would this genoicide also lead to the answer to Judge Kramer's disappearance? Will we finally learn how Nola Kemp figures in all this?

"I wonder if she liked my book." Lockwood's voice cut through both the wailing siren and Max's thoughts.

"Maybe she hasn't had time to read it," was Max's reply.

"Oh, she's read it all right," said Lockwood with confidence and a twinkle. "I can tell when somebody's hooked on me, and she's hooked and she's read it. But Edna's an honest dame and so I'm wondering if she liked it."

Books. Dames. Madame Vilna folded her arms and stared grimly ahead through the windshield. Our world is in chaos and they talk of books and dames. Please, Moses. Let Sylvia Plotkin be alive. I need her to read with me on Saturday night. Shame on you, Vilna. You decry these men for thinking of books and dames in this horrendous emergency, yet you yourself indulge in a similar selfishness. What is happening to all of us? Everybody. The world. Is there nobody who spares a thought for a loved one? If my beloved Plotkin is dead (and perish the thought), how soon will it take Max to become involved with a substitute? (For Sylvia Plotkin a substitute? No such animal exists.)

"You okay?"

Vilna realized with a start that Max was speaking to her. "Do I look disturbed?"

"That was a very painful *oy* you spoke."

"Vilna does not realize she spoke."

"Stop *oy*ing. It doesn't help."

"Me it helps."

The furious wind was no match for a furious Gypsy Marie Rachmaninoff as she cruelly urged the horses forward with curses, threats and a whip.

Her sister Zsa-Zsa pleaded with her to go easy on the animals. "They'll drop in their tracks!" she shouted.

"If they do," shrieked Gypsy Marie, "I'll kill them! I'll render them to glue! Run, you bastards! Run!"

When I lay my hands on you, Piper, when these strong fingers close around your neck, how you shall suffer, you evil man. A pipe broke at the school. *Pfah!* If a pipe broke, why was the basement floor dry when I went looking for you myself last night? At the school all evening except for a trip to the hardware store. *Pfah!* Of course Piper saw Winkle, and Winkle said something to Piper, which was why Piper murdered him. I'm positive Piper murdered him. Winkle must have seen something or found something in Piper's room that made him suspect the old man was somebody else.

And my beloved little Quasimodo. What was it *you* saw? You saw the Piper do something terrible, that's what you saw. I don't need a crystal ball for this. My heart and my reason tell me this. Why else would you have been kidnapped? Or . . . dear God, no. No. Not my little boy. Not my precious child. Not my baby. Piper wouldn't kill *him*. Piper wouldn't harm a *child*. Piper loves children. That *has* to be the one real thing about him. He wove a spell over the entire neighborhood.

The children.

If Piper is a villain, what will this do to the children? Their faith, their trust, their devotion shattered. Who will they ever believe in again? But children are strong. Their wounds will heal. They will survive. My boy will survive. My Quasimodo *has* survived. He has he has he has . . .

"Stop beating those *horses!* You'll have the ASPCA down on my neck."

But Gypsy Marie was deaf to everything except the wind and her throbbing heart.

"Don't touch me! Don't touch me, you *brutes!*" Marianne Kahane sloshed backward as Piper and Chloe burst into the cell, tripped and fell with a splash.

"That wall!" ordered Chloe, pointing past a spluttering Miss Kahane.

"It better be there," growled the Piper. "The building sounds like it's caving in."

They made their way to the wall and frantic fingers searched for a particular stone.

Miss Kahane eyed the open door hungrily. Egress. Escape. Freedom. She pushed herself to her feet, and with one wary eye on the hunters, slowly edged her way toward the door.

"I found it!" cried Piper. "I found it!" He clawed at a loose rock in the wall as Chloe fought a surging wave of triumphal dizziness.

"Hurry, darling, hurry," she urged.

I'm free! I'm free! Miss Kahane darted down the dank, dingy hall toward the stone stairs that led to freedom. Soon she was clambering up the stairs and reached the storm-darkened first-floor hallway. She heard wind and sirens and the bell and a groaning house and a clatter of horses' hoofs, and just as she reached the door to the street, it flung open and Max Van Larsen brandishing a gun came storming in, followed by Lockwood, several policemen and Madame Vilna.

"Down there! Down there!" shrieked the hysterical Miss Kahane. "The second cell on the left. Chloe Grace and a crazy man wearing a woman's clothes! They're mad mad mad, I tell you, mad mad mad." And in a torrent of tears she flung herself against the ample bosom of an astonished Madame Vilna.

Lockwood led three policemen to the subterranean cellar as Max headed upstairs.

"Quasimodo! *Quasimodo!*"

Gypsy Marie Rachmaninoff came tearing in, followed by Zsa-Zsa, Ionesco and a colorful assortment of tribe members.

"Stay down there!" shouted Max from the upper landing. "Madame Vilna! Get them out of here! The place is coming down!"

A section of second-story balcony tore loose and crashed down into the vestry.

"Out!" shouted Vilna in a voice that was a storm all its own. *"Every-*bod-*eeeee* ououououout!"

Marianne Kahane was the first to need no prompting. She tore past Madame Vilna, down the ten stone steps, and raced along the path to the gate. Goodness! All these police! All these gypsies! And I must look a sight!

"The bell tower!" shouted a policeman as the disheveled Miss Kahane ran past him. "The bell tower's crumbling!"

"Sylvia!" screamed Edna St. Thomas Shelley. "The wall's crumbling!"

"Quasi!" cried Sylvia. "Get behind me!"

The three cowered in fear behind the steamer trunk, crouching low as the section of wall that held the door collapsed in a cloud of stone and dust. With it went a section of ceiling, and the gaping hole revealed the clanging bell and the swaying tower directly overhead.

Sylvia raised her head cautiously. "The door's gone!" She grabbed Quasimodo's hand. "Follow me!" Edna St. Thomas Shelley was not a follower. She made it to the hall before the other two, struggling over jagged, protruding sections of collapsed wall. Sylvia came next, releasing Quasimodo's hand as she felt herself tripping over a piece of stone. As she fell she heard a grinding, overpowering noise behind her, and from a corner of her eye, as she frantically struggled to get back to her feet, she could see the floor of the cell beginning to cave in.

"Jump, Quasimodo! Jump!" she shouted.

Quasimodo jumped as the floor caved in beneath him. He jumped with hands outstretched, and they clung to the first thing they contacted. He held the bell rope and swayed back and forth like a circus acrobat as Sylvia realized, with a sinking feeling, there was no way to reach him.

"Sylvia! Sylvia!" screamed Edna. "The other wall's going! Run, you damn fool, run!"

"The boy!" yelled Sylvia. "We can't leave the boy!"

"There's no way to reach him! Save *yourself!*"

The small crowd on the street watched in horror as Quasimodo swung back and forth like a pendulum.

"That's my *boy!*" Gypsy Marie's voice had reached an impossible pitch. "Save my boy! My boy!"

"Call the fire department!" ordered a police sergeant. "Tell them to bring a net!"

A section of ceiling collapsed and missed Van Larsen by a hair's breadth, but he continued up the stairs to the tower. As he rounded a turn he collided with Edna St. Thomas Shelley.

"What kept you?" she gasped.

"Where's Sylvia?"

"Up there! Hurry! She won't leave the kid!"

Max rushed past her.

"Max!" cried Sylvia. "Max! Look out! The wall's tumbling down!"

Max veered sharply as the wall behind which was Ramona's cell began crumbling as though struck by a giant fist. And when the dust cleared away, Max found Sylvia and held her in a tight embrace.

"Max," wept Sylvia, "Max . . . it's Armageddon! And poor Quasi! How can we save poor Quasi?"

"A prett—teeeee girrrlllll . . ."

Arms outstretched, head held high, swaying gracefully, they saw Ramona Grace stepping through the rubble, singing the Irving Berlin melody, seemingly oblivious of the disaster surrounding her.

"Ramona!" cried Sylvia. "It's Ramona!"

"Okay! Okay! Okay!"

They turned and stared at the hunchbacked swinger.

"For crying out loud!" Sylvia couldn't believe either her eyes or her ears. "The kid's enjoying himself!"

"Let's get out of here!" Max grabbed her hand. When they reached Ramona, he grabbed one of her hands and pulled both women with him to what he prayed would still be safety.

Water was filling the subterranean hallway as Lockwood and the three officers came tearing down.

Piper, clutching a tin box in his hands, emerged from the

cell—followed by Chloe—and saw the four men. "Christ!" he shouted.

"This way," said Chloe hastily and led him down the hall to a steel door at the opposite end.

"Stop!" cried Lockwood, but Chloe and the Piper had disappeared through the door.

Chloe led Piper into another passageway, where she pointed to a trapdoor in the floor. "Lift it! It leads to the underground river!"

Madame Vilna clasped her hands with joy as Max appeared in the doorway, followed by Sylvia and a crazy baldheaded lady singing lustily. *Guttenyoo,* thought Madame Vilna, it must be *Ramona.* The poor thing. The poor, poor thing. Scarred, bald and crazy. For sure a most undelectable combination.

Lockwood rushed toward the trapdoor. Reaching it, he looked down and saw a Jacob's ladder that led into a swirling torrent.

"Come back!" he shouted into the yawning opening. "If I don't get you, the water will!" He listened for a reply but none came. "Dammit," he said over his shoulder to the officers, "I'm going after them. And me without rubbers." He holstered his gun and made his way down the teetering ladder.

Chloe choked and spluttered, one hand insecurely clutching the Piper's right shoulder.

"Stop!" she managed to gasp. "Stop! I can't make it!"

"Sure you can, baby . . . don't give up . . ." He swam with his right hand, his left greedily clenched around the tin box.

"I can't . . . I can't . . . I love you . . ."

He felt her grip relax.

"Chloe!"

He turned around and began groping in the water.

"Chloe!"

.   .   .

Lockwood swam with strong athletic strokes.

I'll get you, you bastard, and when I do . . .

And what the hell am I doing like a pregnant salmon swimming upstream? I must be nuts or something. This ain't any ordinary damn sewer. It's a river. A real honest-to-god river. I'm younger and stronger than this bastard. He can't make it, not with that woman he can't.

His hand came in contact with what felt like hair. His fingers took a tight grip on it and Lockwood raised it to eye level.

He stared into Chloe Grace's lifeless eyes.

With alacrity he released his grip and, with renewed strength, continued swimming.

If Chloe Grace is here, can my quarry be far ahead?

"Jump, Quasimodo, jump!"

The net was stretched out under the bell tower. All the boy needed to do was swing to it and release his grip.

Max shouted again, "Jump! Quasi . . . jump! Swing out and let go of the rope!"

"Wheeeeeeeeeeee!"

For the boy, this was no bell rope attached to a soon-to-crumble bell tower. He was swinging on a trapeze in the center ring of a circus, a powerful spotlight following him, and a crowd of thousands holding its breath.

"Gyp," Max shouted to the boy's mother, "do something!"

Gypsy Marie, eyes riveted to her son, stepped forward. Hands on hips and a powerful threat in her voice, she bellowed above the wind, "Gen . . . *ghisssss!*"

The boy relaxed his grip and fell.

The Pied Piper clung to a barred drain, gasping for breath. The water swirled about him, the undertow tearing at his legs, yet tenaciously he clung to both life and the tin box.

The tin box.

The money.

The money that had made him survive those long, dreadful, tedious years of incarceration.

The money.

The dream.

Chloe.

The dream gone.

Chloe gone.

He relaxed his grip on the box and it soon sank.

The money gone.

And then he felt a hand grip his shoulder.

He made no attempt to struggle free. He simply shook his head sadly—a tired, defeated, weary old man.

Said Lockwood as his fingers took a firm grip on the drain bars, "Roscoe Mears, I presume."

CHAPTER XV

That night, after the hurricane had abated, huge police spotlights lit up the roped area surrounding the old church. It was only a shell now, though the section of the tower containing the now-silent bell remained defiantly upright. Quasimodo had dropped safely into the net and from there into his anxious mother's waiting arms. His one-armed cousin had finally emerged from a wagon and nimbly danced a flamenco of thanks around the boy and mother, though one castanet sounded very weak and lonely without its twin. Quasimodo's other cousin surrendered his rifle to a policeman after a series of unsuccessful potshots at the bell. And soon after, the gypsy wagon train wended its way south, welcoming back to the tribe a contrite Gypsy Marie Rachmaninoff and a tearful Quasimodo, who soon lost sight of the handkerchief an equally tearful Sylvia Plotkin was waving.

Lockwood and Roscoe Mears, alias the Pied Piper, had been rescued from the underground river on rubber rafts manned by a sextet of police officers; and then, with a chirruping Ramona,

Roscoe was led to a police wagon that took them to Max's precinct. After being provided with hot coffee and a change of clothes, the Pied Piper and Ramona were interrogated by Max, Lockwood and Herb Roper.

Funny, thought Max as he stared at the tired old man, face now divested of false beard, scar crossing from ear to mouth, face divested of false nose, revealing the true stub, he'll never be Roscoe Mears to me. He'll always be the Pied Piper.

The police secretary waited patiently for the Piper to begin his statement.

Ramona sat strangely quiet. She wore a babushka around her head but the face was bare of any mask, the scarred face for all to see.

"Beauty," she had murmured earlier to Max, "is, after all, only skin-deep. And someplace there must be someone who remembers me as I used to be. Very, very beautiful."

When the old man began speaking, Max felt comfortable again. It was the Piper's voice as he knew it, rich, mellifluous and fruity. All that was missing was a circle of children. He was glad they weren't here. He wished they were illiterate. He dreaded the reactions when they'd read the story in the newspapers. Perhaps one, perhaps just one child, would choose to remember Roscoe Mears as the kindly old Pied Piper.

"I strangled Simon Winkle," the Piper began in a calm, matter-of-fact voice. "I bludgeoned to death Morgan Montescue and Lita Swenson Kramer. These two I murdered disguised as Ramona Grace. I overpowered Ramona Grace in the kitchen of her home yesterday." He looked up at Max and Lockwood. "You two were on the premises when I did it." The eyes were twinkling. "That was the fuss you heard from the kitchen. Everyone was closing in on me. You, Lockwood, and Monty and Simon. I guess if I could have shook the old betting habit, Simon might not have gotten suspicious. But he did get suspicious. He shook down my room at the school and left a note. It wasn't addressed to the Pied Piper, it was addressed to Roscoe

Mears. So I went to his place, and the rest was quite simple. Winkle didn't think for a minute I'd kill him. He let me in. He told me Montescue wanted to see me and make a deal for Ramona's property. I could keep the money if I found it. The money." He shook his head sadly and then continued talking. "I didn't give a damn about the property."

"*My* property. All mine. All mine." Ramona was smiling. She nodded at the Piper and he resumed speaking.

"I just wanted the money and a last chance at some happiness with my wife." Max and Herb Roper exchanged glances. Lockwood's eyes were glued on the Piper. "Chloe was my wife. When I was sent to jail, it was agreed she'd stick to Ramona until I got sprung."

"She threw acid in my face." It was a barely audible whisper. "Over thirty years I've lived with this face."

"Yes," said the Piper, "it was Chloe who disfigured her. But only after Ramona admitted she was in on the frame that landed me in San Quentin."

"I had to keep Chloe with me, though. She had too much on me," interjected Ramona.

Piper resumed talking. "After I killed Winkle, I went through his papers. I found Montescue's address." He laughed. "Shrewd old bugger, living right next door to Lita. I went to his house first, but he wasn't there. I tried Lita's. Two birds with one stone. Monty could have sent me back to jail. I'm sorry about the kid. But he looked in the church window and saw us trussing up Ramona. Chloe and I caught him and locked him up. But I wouldn't have hurt him. I promise you that."

Max nodded

"Is he okay?"

"Yes," said Max. "Gypsy Marie and the boy rejoined the tribe. It seems, like so many of us, they now loathe New York. They're heading south. They're holding their Gyp-In in Miami Beach. What happened to Judge Kramer?"

The Piper turned to Ramona.

She was still smiling. Slowly her eyes moved until they locked with Max's. "He's buried behind the church. Nola Kemp murdered him. Nola was a bad girl. She took his money. She got his property. But Armand was a frightened man. He knew too much. He had decided to go to the police and turn himself in, to try and get a deal and save his own neck. Nola had struggled for years to gain money and power. It's all she dreamt of. And if Armand spilled the beans to the cops, like today, the walls would have come tumbling down. Nola would have none of that, so she stabbed Armand in the kitchen of the old church, with the very knife used to cut the chocolate cake, and then she and Chloe dug a grave next to the other graves and buried him."

She threw back her head and laughed, and when the laughter subsided, she spoke again. "Nola was shrewd. No one knew who she was. No one knew where she came from. She drifted in and out of the theater unseen and undetected, and when the show closed, she disappeared."

"And you have no idea what's become of her?" prodded Max.

"Of course I do!" said Ramona haughtily. "Nola and I are in constant touch. She's still very, very beautiful. Her face isn't covered with ugly scars like mine. Nola is exactly the way she was in the old days."

"Where is she?" asked Max.

"Don't be such a fool, Max," said the Piper with a new twinkle in his eyes. "I thought you were too smart for a put-on. You want Nola Kemp? You're looking at Nola Kemp. Ramona . . . Nola . . . the same person."

Max heard an intake of breath, and then realized it was his own.

Ramona was laughing again. "Here she is, boys!" She now stood up with arms outstretched toward the detectives. "Here's Nola Kemp! Ain't she stunning?"

. . .

There was a babble of excited conversation in Sylvia's apartment, contributed by the hostess, Max Van Larsen, Burton Lockwood, Edna St. Thomas Shelley and Madame Vilna. Finally Sylvia's voice cut like a well-honed scythe, and she won their attention.

"Well, if I hadn't been watching that old movie on TV this afternoon the Piper starred in and heard him say, *I, said the Demon . . .*"

"The eyes," swiftly interrupted Madame Vilna. "I recognized the *eyes . . .*"

"Urmph," said Lockwood, and Edna rewarded him with a winning smile.

"More cake anybody?" asked Sylvia. She found a taker in Lockwood.

"Now then, you two," said Edna, meaning Max and Sylvia, "start collating your facts and get to work on that book about the Grace Sisters. The trial's going to be a honey, and it's about time," she added slyly, "you two carried your collaboration a little further."

Sylvia nervously patted her hair.

Vilna winked broadly at Lockwood.

Max rubbed sweaty palms against his trousers.

"Well?" insisted Edna.

Max leaned back in his seat as his eyes found Sylvia's. "Sylvia baby," he said, "at the risk of sending you into shock, do you suppose you could heat me up some of your chicken soup?"

"Oh, Max," whispered Sylvia, "dear Max," and burst into uncontrollable tears.

GEORGE BAXT
His Life and Hard Times

On a Monday afternoon, June 11, 1923, George Baxt was born on a kitchen table in Brooklyn.

He was nine when his first published work appeared in the Brooklyn *Times-Union*. He received between two and five dollars for each little story or poem the paper used.

His first play was produced when he was eighteen. It lasted one night.

Mr. Baxt has been a propagandist for Voice of America, a press agent, and an actor's agent. He has written extensively for stage, screen, and television. During stays in England in the fifites, he wrote a number of films *(Circus of Horrors; Horror Hotel; Burn, Witch, Burn)* which are now staples of late night television.

His first novel, A QUEER KIND OF DEATH, was published in 1966. His other novels include SWING LOW, SWEET HARRIET; A PARADE OF COCKEYED CREATURES; TOPSY AND EVIL; "I!" SAID THE DEMON; PROCESS OF ELIMINATION; THE DOROTHY PARKER MURDER CASE; and most recently THE ALFRED HITCHCOCK MURDER CASE.

Mr. Baxt lives in New York, is a bachelor, and is devoted to his VCR.

THE LIBRARY OF CRIME CLASSICS®

THE BEST IN MYSTERY—
PAST AND PRESENT
BACKLIST

George Baxt
THE ALFRED HITCHCOCK
MURDER CASE $5.95
THE DOROTHY PARKER
MURDER CASE
"I!" SAID THE DEMON
A QUEER KIND OF DEATH
A PARADE OF COCKEYED
CREATURES
SWING LOW, SWEET HARRIET

Anthony Boucher
NINE TIMES NINE

Caryl Brahms & S.J. Simon
A BULLET IN THE BALLET
MURDER A LA STROGANOFF
SIX CURTAINS FOR
STROGANOVA

Christianna Brand
CAT AND MOUSE

Max Brand
THE NIGHTFLOWER

John Dickson Carr
BELOW SUSPICION
THE BURNING COURT
DEATH TURNS THE TABLES
HAG'S NOOK
HE WHO WHISPERS
THE HOUSE AT SATAN'S
ELBOW
THE PROBLEM OF THE
GREEN CAPSULE
THE SLEEPING SPHINX
THE THREE COFFINS
TILL DEATH DO US PART

Carroll John Daly
MURDER FROM THE EAST

Lillian De La Torre
DR. SAM: JOHNSON, DETECTOR
THE DETECTIONS OF
DR. SAM: JOHNSON
THE EXPLOITS OF DR. SAM:
JOHNSON, DETECTOR $5.95
THE RETURN OF DR. SAM:
JOHNSON, DETECTOR

Carter Dickson
THE JUDAS WINDOW

**Dashiell Hammett &
Alex Raymond**
SECRET AGENT X–9, 6" × 10", $9.95

Paul Gallico
THE ABANDONED $5.95

James Gollin
ELIZA'S GALLIARDO
THE PHILOMEL FOUNDATION

Richard Hull
THE MURDER OF MY AUNT

Victoria Lincoln
A PRIVATE DISGRACE $5.95
LIZZIE BORDEN BY DAYLIGHT

Barry N. Malzberg
UNDERLAY

Margaret Millar
AN AIR THAT KILLS
ASK FOR ME TOMORROW
BANSHEE